A Shot At Love

A Curvy Girl Romance

Kay Sinclair

A Love Note

To all the gorgeous women out there with thick thighs, soft stomachs, and ample asses...

Your body is a triumph. A masterpiece. A blessing.

You are worthy of whatever you choose for yourself in your life—and don't let anyone tell you otherwise.

CONTENTS

1

LANDON

I'M HEADING INTO BATTLE. Or at least, that's how it feels. My lipstick, my armor. My hair, curled into soft waves, my helmet. Manicured nails, my daggers.

Okay, maybe I'm being a little dramatic ... it's just a first date. With a stranger from the internet. And I need to get in there and get it over with already.

I check my lipstick in the mirror, brush away a nearly invisible speck of makeup beneath my eye, and take a deep breath. My fluttering heartbeat is an erratic mess.

Stepping out of the car and onto the street, I steel myself against the light rain that never seems to stop here in the Pacific Northwest and make my way to the front door of Sullivan's Place.

I've only lived in Temptation Falls for a few months, and though I've driven by here several times, I've never been in before. I haven't really made many friends yet, working from home and all.

Thankfully, there's no line to get in. There is, however, an elderly couple walking my way down the street. The husband's arm loops through his wife's bent elbow, helping her when she staggers a little on the uneven pavement. The look she gives him radiates true love, and my heart aches. It's the sweetest thing I've ever seen.

"Are you coming in here?" I call, putting my hand to my forehead as a visor against the drizzle. The man looks up and nods fervently. I wait for a moment until they arrive, then heave the heavy door open to let them in first. They thank me, the woman beaming, and I follow them in.

I'm surprised to see how crowded the dim bar is. It's a Thursday night in a small town, but evidently, Thirsty Thursday is in full effect and this is the place to go. A huge, glossy wooden bar spans almost the entire room to my right, wrapping around from the windows at the front all the way to the back wall, where it ends with a saloon-style hinged door. Bottles upon bottles of liquor span the backlit shelves on the wall behind the bar. To my left, a combination of cherry-red leather booths and dark-stained wood tables overflow with people drinking beer and enjoying a good time. There's a lone pool table in the back, crowded with young men, and a few dart boards up on the wall.

I instantly love it, and it takes the edge off my nerves. I scan the faces around the room, looking at each person sitting at the bar, but I don't see Mike anywhere. At least, I don't think I do. It's always hard to tell with online dating. Which, in my opinion, is the worst of all the dating types.

And yet here I am.

Mike is my newest attempt at the world of online romance. Based on our chats, he seems nice enough, but it's tricky to judge. He, at least, said he liked my photos. And finding men to swipe right when you're a plus-size woman isn't the easiest thing.

I know, logically, that tons of women are curvy and drop-dead gorgeous. And I'd never tell another human they don't deserve love because of how they look. Even though I'm actively working to embrace my body, it's just tough when the world screams that fat is a problem to be fixed.

For years, I've promised myself that I'll start dating when I lose thirty pounds, or when I can wear a size ten, or when a large top doesn't fit like a crop top ... but never as I am right now.

But that's complete and total bullshit, isn't it?

I just didn't fully realize it until my spin instructor said something that shook me to my bones.

What would you do if you were three times more confident and three times less scared?

That was the moment I decided to be bold and do the damn thing. I downloaded the apps and started swiping. I'm not waiting for external approval before going for what I want anymore. Because honestly, I want to be in love. And I'm not going to let fear stand in my way for another second longer.

I walk to an empty bar stool and perch. There's no sign of Mike anywhere yet.

"What can I get for you?" a deep voice says, grabbing my attention.

I turn and see a large hand splayed on the glossy wood of the bar. My eyes travel up. My stomach swoops as I take in the bartender.

Holy moly.

His eyes, framed by black lashes, are so deeply brown that the pupils are nearly invisible. Dark, slashing eyebrows make his gaze hawklike. Magnetic. Soul piercing.

A short beard covers his broad jaw, and his dark and wavy hair is pushed back from his face. Not gelled and coiffed like so many guys do lately—more like he's raked it back so many times that it's simply given up on falling back down. My fingers twitch, longing to tangle in those curls.

The longer I hold his gaze, the hotter the spark in my chest grows.

Finally, I remember he's waiting for an answer. "Pinot grigio, if you have it. Or another white, please," I say after a breath.

The bartender nods. When he turns to grab a wine glass, I shake my head, trying to clear the haze that's passed over me. And I can't help it … my eyes stray down to his slim-fit jeans. But there's nothing slim about him otherwise. He's tall, well over six feet, and built. Absolutely jacked, to be more specific. Broad, muscled shoulders stretch the seams of his well-worn charcoal-colored flannel.

Now *this* is the kind of man who gets numbers alongside every single bill, along with some nice, beefy tips from the female customers. Probably some of the men, too.

And I get it. Because if I could have the universe design me my absolutely perfect physical type, this man would be *freaking it.*

I shake my head again. Why am I even thinking about this? I really need to rein in my wandering mind. And my spiking hormones.

Mike's handsome too, just in a more clean-cut way.

My head on a swivel, I check the door and do a quick scan of the room. Still no sign of my date. And no messages on my phone. I worry my lower lip. He's only a few minutes late, though, no biggie.

"Here you go. Wanna keep the tab open?" The bartender is back with my drink, which he slides over. His voice is all gruff and gravel, the words almost clipped, like he isn't used to conversation.

"Um, open, please," I reply, passing over my card. He twirls it between his long fingers. I can feel his eyes on me like heat as I glance at the door again. It's either that or start drooling right here on the bar if I look at him for too much longer.

"Waiting for a date?"

I turn my head back to him so fast I almost get whiplash. "What?"

His face is unreadable as he looks at me for a moment, brow furrowed slightly. He steps away to file my card at the register, and then faces me once more. He leans against the back counter and crosses his muscled arms. "You've just got that look. Didn't mean anything by it."

I take a deep breath. "Well, if it's that obvious ... yeah, first date. I'm a little nervous."

He grunts but doesn't say anything.

Why is my finger tapping the glass so obsessively? Have I always done this? Why can't I stop? I down a heavy swallow of the wine and let the strong flavor overwhelm my senses for a moment.

He still watches me like a hawk, and I take another sip, looking up through my eyelashes at him as I do. My skin flushes under the weight of his gaze. Finally, he says, "Your date is a fucking lucky man. But if he tries anything, you get me, okay? I'll take care of you. And I'll take care of him." His final words promise something dark and dangerous.

I stare, trying to process not only his words but also his intent.

Your date is a fucking lucky man.

I'll take care of you.

After a moment, I nod. "Thank you," I say, and an exhale of relief comes through in my voice.

To be honest, my last online date didn't go too well, which might explain some of my soaring levels of pre-date anxiety. But the idea that this giant of a man is here, offering to help me if I need, wraps me in a sense of safety I didn't know was missing. And it's not just that—heat spreads like wildfire in my chest, through my heart. Everything about this man seems to be lighting me up.

Maybe he's just trying to be nice to the solo girl at the bar, but at the moment, I don't care. I can feel his protective energy from across the bar, and I drink it in like I'm dying for water in the desert.

Before he walks away to help another customer, I swear I hear him growl low in his throat. I swallow hard. As soon as he leaves, I can't help but want him to come back.

To distract myself from my unbidden thoughts—I'm here to meet a different man, after all—I sip my wine, performing the now-familiar visual circuit around the room. Nothing. Though I do see some women staring markedly at the bar, and I presume, the sexy bartender.

Honestly, I can't blame them. I keep sneaking glances at him from beneath my lashes. At one point, he rolls up his sleeves, revealing the edges of a dark tattoo. I wonder how far up the tattoo goes, what it depicts. Does it stretch across his chest too? What other tattoos are hidden beneath that inconspicuous flannel?

I mean, come on. He's like catnip for the ladies.

But at this point, despite the view, I'm getting antsy. Mike is twenty minutes late. I finally give in to my twitchiness and shoot him a quick text asking if he wants me to grab him a drink. If that isn't a subtle call for an ETA, then I don't know what is.

The minutes pass. No text back. No wine left in my glass.

Prickling heat blooms across my cheeks when it finally sinks in.

He's standing me up.

Or maybe it's worse than that. Maybe he came in, saw me, decided there was no way in hell he wanted to be on a date with me, and promptly left the building.

I grab my glass with shaking fingers only to remember it's empty already. I stare up at the neon lights on the wall of fancy alcohol, trying to stop the tears I can feel welling up. This is humiliating beyond belief.

Worse, the hot bartender is going to know I've been stood up. There's no need to protect the damsel in distress when her date doesn't even show.

Someone bumps into me, and I nearly fall off my stool. A stunning woman shoulders into the open space at the bar. She leans forward. Long hair swings around her shoulders, and her thin frame is just like every celebrity I see in every single magazine. Her lips pout in a sly smile as the bartender approaches. He smiles back.

I can tell you right now if that smile had been focused on me, my knees would've given out.

But it isn't.

They chat as he readies a cocktail. These are the kind of people who fall in love, not me.

My throat closes up. I gotta get out of here.

I grab a twenty from my wallet and throw it next to my empty glass. I slide off my barstool and barely make it out into the darkening night before the tears start to fall.

2

VAUGHN

THE RAG HITS ME smack in the face. I jerk back, startled, and whip my head to the side. Aaron is there, cackling.

"Wow, you really are on another planet right now, Vaughn. Did you hear anything I said?" he asks.

"Yeah, I mean, you were talking about ... something interesting, right?" I give my friend a crooked, guilty smile. I wasn't listening at all.

"Dude, I was asking you about that blonde from earlier, the one that wouldn't leave you alone. Did you get her number? She was smoking hot."

It takes me a second to remember who Aaron is talking about. When the memory sifts into place, I roll my eyes. That girl pressed me for free drinks for ages, hoping her big tits and puffed-up lips would pay the bill. She did slip me her number too, but it went right in the bin. I appreciated the hefty tip she left me, though.

I need every cent I can get right now—my dad's been calling and calling, ready for his next installment.

I grind my teeth at the thought. Needing something to do with my hands, I grab the rag Aaron tossed at me and start wiping down the bar. It's almost two in the morning, and we're finally closing Sullivan's down for the night. I can't wait to go to bed, even if it's only for a few hours. This is my tenth straight day working, and even though I'm loath to admit it, I'm exhausted. I wish I could take tomorrow off, but it's not in the cards. I won't get a break until Monday.

"Well?" Aaron presses me.

"I wasn't interested."

He groans. "Youth is wasted on the young."

I give him a look. "You're two years older than me."

"Yeah, and I'm enjoying my youth far more than you! Me, I seize the day, carpe diem and all that. You just work and work. And work."

"You're my boss. You should be happy that I work all the time. And you know I have to pay off this loan. I can't deal with that asshole breathing down my neck, guilt-tripping me anymore."

Five years ago, I made the mistake of going back to school—and the even bigger mistake of asking my father to help finance it. I set the arrangement right from the start. I'd pay him back with interest, just a bit less than the bank would charge. At the time, I thought it was a great deal. Better rates than a federal loan, at least. And once I graduated, I was sure to pull down a six-figure salary plus benefits that would make paying him back a breeze.

Only, things didn't go quite as planned.

About two years into dumping an ungodly amount of money into tuition, books, late-night pizzas, and room and board, I was more miserable than I'd been in my entire life. I didn't want to get out of bed, didn't care enough to open my textbooks and study. I started hating everyone and everything. I couldn't fathom a future where I spent my life in a courtroom or perusing dusty tombs looking for specific case laws and penal codes.

When I made the decision to drop out and find a new path, my dad was pissed. He said the loan payments needed to start immediately, even though I didn't have a job yet—and he's been hounding me for bimonthly payments ever since, dangling the debt over my head.

Really, I should've seen it coming. We aren't close, my dad and I, and for good reason. He struggled with a gambling addiction when I was a kid. Our rental houses got smaller and more run down every year, and he started spending less and less time with us in them. My mom finally threw him out after she found out about his string of torrid affairs when I was in high school.

When my mom passed away when I was nineteen, he didn't even bother to attend the funeral. I arranged it all myself.

Thankfully, Mom had been thrifty beyond belief, squirreling away her own secret bank account after years of watching Dad lose money. She left me enough to pay for college, but it didn't stretch much beyond that. After a few years of working odd jobs and struggling to find a career with only an English degree to arm me, I thought going back to school would be a smart investment.

I had kept in touch with Dad on and off, and in the years after my parent's divorce, it seemed like he pulled it together and made something of himself. Which is why I took that risk and asked him for help.

Just goes to show what happens when you let your guard down and trust someone.

"I know, your old man's a dick. I get it," Aaron says, jogging me out of my dark thoughts. "But don't let him take all the fun out of your life. Once in a while, you've gotta take a day or two off and actually enjoy yourself. The bar will still be waiting for you when you get back."

"I'll have fun once I can write that last check and finally be done paying off this damned loan. I never should've taken it in the first place. And look where it got me—I'm a law school dropout whose best skill is blending fruity cocktails for girls at bachelorette parties."

"And that is exactly the skill I love you for. We make a killing with those parties." Aaron grins and elbows me lightly in the ribs. "And that said, next time you get a number, please try to take advantage of it. Life's short. Don't waste it being angry with someone who's not worth it."

Without waiting for my response, Aaron hefts two bursting trash bags and ducks out the door to the alley.

I just shake my head.

But truth be told, I can't get a different woman out of my mind. Not that simpering bleached blonde, but the other one. The woman with dark blonde hair and piercing blue eyes. Curves for days.

I haven't experienced such a surge of possessiveness, of *want*, for years. Ever, if I'm being honest. As soon as she looked me in the eyes, all I'd been able to think was, *Mine.*

That moment when she chewed on her lower lip and glanced at me when she thought I wasn't looking ... I thought I might spontaneously combust. Even just thinking about her now, I'm starting to feel a rush of things I shouldn't be feeling in the workplace.

What else can those lips do? How would those soft, luscious curves feel under my rough fingertips?

A flash of anger surges through me, cutting off my rapidly escalating thoughts, and I grip the rag tighter.

I'm pretty sure her date stood her up—or at least, I assume that's what happened. She waited for ages by herself, looking so sweet and nervous, and then she just disappeared. She left cash on the bar even though she had a card on file.

What kind of asshole leaves someone waiting like that? Especially a drop-dead knockout like her? I hate guys like that, guys like my father who don't give a damn about other people's feelings.

But I must admit, I'm a little relieved I didn't have to see her flirt with some other man. I don't even know her name, but I'm pretty sure I would have broken something if I had to watch someone else make her smile.

I think I got my foot in the door, though, with my comment about her date being a fucking lucky man. And telling her I'd take care of her. I never say shit like that to customers, but it slipped out before I could stop it. It felt *right.* And it was true. I'd take care of her—and I'd absolutely crush any man who hurt her. She seemed surprised by my words, but grateful too.

The one bright spot in this night is that there's still the chance, the slimmest chance, that I might get to see her again when she comes to pick up her credit card. Though these days, it seems like half the people who leave cards just never come back for them. And I'd have to be working at the same time ... and be the one at the bar when she walks in.

A guy can dream though, right?

My phone buzzes, and I start. Who the hell would be calling me this late—or rather, early?

I tug it out of my jeans pocket and glance at the caller ID. Fuck.

At least this will get my head out of the gutter.

"Dad," I answer, my voice flat.

"Thought you'd be up," he says by way of a greeting. "Just want to confirm you're on track for your next payment this week."

"Yep. You'll have it. Just like always." My fist clenches.

"Just need to confirm it. It's hard to know about the reliability of a dropout who works in a dive bar. I'll expect it in my account next week, then." His words are sharp. No questions about my life, no interest in anything besides the payment. After he drags the grunt of affirmation out of me, the call ends.

Bastard.

I force myself to take a deep breath so I don't do what I'd *rather* do right now, which is punch the wall.

I use all my mental willpower to return to my closing duties and push the conversation out of my head. In its place rises the image of that gorgeous curvy goddess again. It's like she's taken root in my skull.

A muscle jumps in my jaw. I really need to focus. I might never see her again, so it's no use pining after her. Even if I *do* see her, it's not like anything can happen, no matter how much my mind wants to play out the potential scenarios. I have bigger things to worry about. I can't stop working, can't take time off to be with a woman in any real sort of way. And what woman would want to be with someone who works twenty-four seven and has no money?

Aaron and I finish closing down the bar in silence before walking out to the dimly lit back alley together. Our Harleys share a parking spot, mine a sleek black machine that I've rebuilt and tailored into an absolutely classic stunner. Aaron's, on the other hand, is a lurid cherry-red monstrosity that makes me flinch every time I see it, even in the murky dark.

We've been riding together for years, us and a few other guys who enjoy fast machines and a bit of a thrill. Most of them actually work at Sullivan's with Aaron and me. But of all the guys in our crew, Aaron is the most like a brother to me. A big, goofy brother who never lets the world phase him, even when the really bad shit happens. I've known him since high school. He's the person I'm closest to in my life, really, with Mom gone and Dad being, well, himself.

As I strap on my helmet, Aaron says, "Want to get out for a ride tomorrow before our shifts? The weather's supposed to be clear."

I'm grateful he doesn't bring up our conversation from earlier again. "Nah, man. I'm watching Katya's kids for the morning."

"Again? You've been taking them a lot lately."

"Yeah, well, she pays me for it. I'm basically the fun uncle slash nanny," I say.

"No, she *barely* and only *occasionally* pays you for it. And wait, are you their uncle though? Your cousin's kids would be ... your second cousins? Nieces and nephews? How the hell does that work? I always get confused."

"I think they're technically my cousins once removed, but we stick with 'Uncle Vaughn' for simplicity's sake."

"Makes sense. But what doesn't make sense is why, on your morning off, you're picking up even more work. Did you hear anything I said earlier?"

So much for him not bringing it up.

"Heard and noted," I reply as I shut my helmet visor with a snap.

I can actually *feel* Aaron rolling his eyes at me, even though his helmet blocks his face. He's just trying to help, but I've got a mission. A morning with the kids—even after only five hours of sleep—followed by my shift at the bar is going to get me one step closer to my goal. I can power through it. I'm so close. Well, not *that* close, but I'm getting there.

"Maybe one day you'll realize just how wise I really am and listen to me, for once," Aaron says in a resigned tone as he pulls on his riding gloves. He punches me lightly on my leather-padded arm. "See you tomorrow."

He takes off into the night on his cherry-red eyesore.

I rev my own bike and turn in the other direction, heading for my apartment. I try to stay focused, but the road simply can't compete with the memory of those blue eyes gazing back at me from across the bar.

3

LANDON

Friday passes in a hangover haze.

I may have indulged in a few too many glasses of wine after the disastrous date-that-never-was. I managed to avoid full-on meltdown mode, telling myself it was no use crying (too much) over a man I'd never even met who, for all I know, could be into taxidermy. But today I'm paying for the two—three?—glasses of wine that I nursed during my pre-bed moping session.

Just once, I want to be *that* girl. The one the man shows up for, without fail. The one he fights for. But I can't even get an internet date to show, let alone woo me.

I stare foggily at my computer, trying to shake my glum mood and focus.

When I dreamed of being a writer as a kid, I didn't imagine that so much of my work would be dedicated to plugging Google search terms into blog posts. The story matters less to my clients than the ranking. But they pay me good money for it, so who am I to complain?

When I finally finish my work, I email it off and let out a sigh of relief. Just in the nick of time. I grab the giant container of homemade cupcakes I baked yesterday and hop in the car.

When I moved to Temptation Falls for a fresh start, I decided I wanted to make my dream of writing books a reality, so I found a novel writing group to join. I've only been to three sessions so far, but I'm getting to know the other writers, and it's so fun being around other creatives who laugh and joke about the writing problems that plague us all. It makes it all less daunting, in a way. And it's a nice spot of connection on a pretty empty social calendar.

I've made it scarcely a mile in the direction of the library when the gas light flickers on in my dash.

My old sedan is my baby, but it's also a clunker. When I first bought the car years ago, my dad would joke that I only got five miles per gallon in the thing. And honestly, he wasn't far off.

I head to the gas station that's a few blocks away, pull in, and park. I dig out my wallet and flip it open. Except ...

Oh no.

I search through my wallet again, then my bag.

Where the hell is my credit card?

Stolen? Lost? Dropped?

I groan and smack a hand to my forehead when the memory surfaces.

The bar. I gave that sexy, broody bartender my card to put on file, didn't I? But when Mike didn't show, I completely forgot and paid in cash. The *last* of my cash, of course. So not only do I not have a credit card, I can't even get gas.

Worse, to get my card back, I'm going to have to face the bartender who knows I was stood up.

This is really not my week.

Swearing under my breath, I leave the gas station and drive to the library. That's a tomorrow-me problem.

All it takes is a quick game of this week's icebreaker—rose and thorn—for me to spill all the details of my date disaster to the group.

The other writers fill the air with dramatic expletives, calling for Mike's head ... and other, more sensitive parts.

Beatrice, an elderly Scottish woman wrapped in at least three shawls and with glasses so thick all it would take was a sunny day to start a fire, calls for quiet. "I think we can all agree that sweet Landon here dodged a bullet with that oaf! But let's look on the bright side. Landon, do ye have a rose for the week that might help offset this thorn?"

I pause, biting into a cupcake to give myself a moment to think. Do I have a rose? I can't think of one.

As the frosting swirls around my tongue, though, the bartender's face surfaces in my thoughts.

Your date is a fucking lucky man.

Such a small thing, but the memory sends heat from my ears all the way down to my toes.

"Well," I hedge, trying to regulate my hormones, "there was this bartender last night. He complimented me. So, I guess that felt nice? Sorry, is that a lame rose to share? I can try to think of something else."

"There's another man in the mix? That's the perfect rose! When are you going back to talk to him?" Beatrice asks.

"What? I'm not!" I protest. "Oh God, except I need to go back and get my credit card. I left it there."

"It's the perfect meet-cute!" shouts Gene, a freckled kid in his late teens who's all pointy elbows and knobby knees.

I quickly shake my head. "No, you don't understand. This guy is so out of my league. He was probably just being nice—"

Maggie interrupts me. "Girl, stop that self-deprecating stuff right this instant. Men don't give compliments they don't mean. Unless it's to their wives, of course, in which case they're a required aspect of the marriage contract.

Remember that, babe." She looks sideways at her fiancé, the best-selling sci-fi author sitting next to her, and winks.

"Hey, I *always* mean my compliments—" Caden gets out before Maggie cuts him off with a shooshing gesture. He rolls his eyes, but a small smile still plays on his lips as he stares at her.

"Yes, Maggie's right," Gene says, nodding sagely.

"You guys don't get it. He's like the hero you see in the movies. The one who dates model heiresses who never wear sweats or eat carbs. You should've seen the woman hitting on him. But anyway, that's enough about me! Maya, you're up next, right?" I try to shift the focus toward the gorgeous brunette at my side.

Beatrice leans forward, shawls swinging and knocking a pencil to the ground. "Sweet Landon, even if that man was just being nice, I'm getting a tingle about this whole thing. I think there's a story a'brewing."

"Oooh," Maggie squeals. "Beatrice has a super-sense for stories! It's how I finished my last one."

I raise my eyebrows.

"Yes, I'm sure of it," Beatrice continues. "You need to get back to that bar. Find the story."

"My stories aren't set in bars. What could I possibly write about there?"

"Dearest Landon, I'm going to throw a harsh truth out on the table, but it's not because I don't love you. You came to us because you haven't been able to finish a book, isn't that right?" Beatrice asks me, her Scottish accent transforming her voice into lilting music.

"Yes," I mumble.

"Not a single thing wrong with that. Lord knows how many writers have the same trouble. But maybe this is the secret ingredient that's been missing, if you know what I mean."

I don't.

"Maybe trying something a bit different will unlock that writing muse. Nothing wrong with giving something a chance, aye?" Beatrice gives me a kind smile. "And for the record, any man would be lucky to be with you. Don't you ever forget it."

Everyone at the table nods vigorously. I rapidly blink away the unexpected burn of tears.

Maya grabs another cupcake from the plate in the middle of the table and rests her free hand on my arm. "Actually, I think there's more than unlocking the muse that needs to happen here. I think it's time for *you* to get swept up in your own main character energy."

"Huh?"

"Girl, you're *incredible*. We all love having you here, you're kind to literally every single person you meet, you're whip-smart, you make us laugh, you bring us cupcakes, and you're a knockout. If you were to write a romance novel, you could be your own main character! That's the kind of energy you need to start bringing. If you were the main character in your story, if you were the badass protagonist—or the badass author I know you want to be—what would you do? What would you go after?" Maya asks.

I don't answer. Isn't this the same thing the spin instructor encouraged? *What would you do if you were three times more confident and three times less scared?*

"Just think about it," Maya finishes, licking frosting off her fingertip and for all the world looking like a curvy goddess from a Renaissance painting.

On Saturday morning, I wake up feeling infinitely better. My coffee smells amazing, the sun is peeking out from behind the clouds, and—best of all—I feel inspired.

I'm itching to build a new world, play with characters, and get into the flow of my work again.

Plus, Maya's words keep floating back to me.

If you were the main character in your story, if you were the badass protagonist—or the badass author I know you want to be—what would you do?

I drain my coffee and make up my mind.

Today, I'm trying something new. I'm going to kick off a new book in a new genre—and this time, I'm going to finish the damn thing. And that's not all, world! I'm going to test out this whole "main character energy" thing too.

Landon Davis is back in business.

Edit: Once I get my stupid credit card back, I'm back in business. Insert power pose here!

But after showering and putting on my makeup, I stare into my closet as though it were an empty refrigerator during a late afternoon caffeine crash. I need an outfit that screams "I'm a successful badass author!"

Looking the part is half the battle, right?

Unbidden, another thought floats to the surface of my mind. *And what outfit will make the sexy bartender look twice?*

I can't help the flush that creeps up my neck. Why does my brain keep going back to that man? I don't even know his name, and yet here he is, taking up all my mental space.

Another memory jolts me. The dream I had last night. He was in it. Boy, was he ever in it. His big hands played a significant role too ...

A shiver races down my spine.

I need to get ahold of myself. He's probably not even working today—and if he is, if he even remembers me, he'll remember me as the pathetic girl who gets stood up on her dates. I don't stand a chance.

Yet, I can't shake the thought of those sexy dark eyes and that growl.

I slip into a pair of dark wash jeans that hug my curves, a blouse that drops to near-dangerous lows in the front, and a tailored leather jacket that I hardly ever wear. It never quite feels like me—but today, it's just the thing. It's time to push out of my comfort zone, be the Landon I *want* to be. The Landon who can take on the world.

After throwing on a heeled pair of ankle boots, I inspect myself in the mirror. The outfit is chic. But my eyes come to rest on my stomach, not quite camouflaged by the blouse and jacket. The momentary confidence that came with the outfit fizzles.

I hate it, the constant wavering between wanting to feel beautiful, feeling beautiful for a moment, and then feeling my insecurities creep back in like a spreading vine. Normally, I'd change. But not today.

Badass Author Landon loves her curves. She isn't worried about someone seeing the luscious rolls of her stomach or the sensual heft of her hips.

So today, I choose to see myself as I *want* to be seen.

I gather up my notebook, laptop, and book on story structure. I debate putting it all into a backpack but decide to go with my favorite purse instead and just carry the rest. No point in ruining the look when I only have to get it from the car into the coffee shop.

It's just plain bad luck that I'm still a mile away from Sullivan's when my old sedan splutters to a stop, giving me only moments to pull over to the shoulder to avoid blocking the entire road.

No gas.

Well, I misjudged that one completely. And without my credit card, I can't do anything to fix my current dilemma.

Walking to the bar it is, then.

Not wanting to leave my things in the car, I pick up my laptop and books to carry with me. I can always stop at a coffee shop on the way back from the bar.

Thankfully, it's a beautiful day for a little stroll, though typically, I prefer to stroll without my hands full and with more comfortable shoes on … and in a place where loud motorcycles don't drive slowly by, their engines roaring so loudly I can't hear myself think.

Who would've thought the small town of Temptation Falls had so many motorcycles?

Eventually, the bar's back alley comes into sight, a shortcut to the main road where the entrance is. I thank the heavens that this walk is over. My feet are aching like none other.

The sight of two huge motorcycles and two leather-clad riders in the alley, one bike idling with its rider still sitting upon it, stops me dead in my tracks. Both men wear helmets, and they turn their masked faces to stare at me. A chill creeps up my back. There's something about being a woman in an alley with two strange men that's always going to be a little disconcerting.

But it's the middle of the day, and the bar—and my lost credit card—are so close. I really don't want to have to walk all the way around the block in these damn shoes. This way, I only have to go another twenty yards, and then I can finally move on with my day and get to writing.

I clutch my computer and books to my chest like a shield, holding my head high.

Main character energy.

As I step closer, one of the men pulls off his helmet and combs roughly through his wavy hair with his free hand. He turns and meets my gaze, dark eyes and slashing eyebrows giving him a focused intensity that makes me shiver.

Sexy bartender.

Of course he rides a motorcycle.

My heart skips, and though I blush furiously, I keep walking.

The second man removes his helmet to reveal a grinning face, wheat-colored hair, and a clean-shaven jaw. He shrugs off his jacket next, showing off absolutely jacked arms.

There's gotta be something in the water—or the beer—at Sullivan's Place. It turns all men into massive babes.

I turn the corner onto the main road and slip inside the front door of the bar, looking around. It's amazing how different the vibe is without the patrons crowding every table. It's actually really nice.

With a sigh of relief, I drop my laptop and books onto the glossy counter and slide onto a barstool to wait, giving my poor feet a break.

But as I wait, heat begins to burn across my cheeks and down my chest. I can't stop it. The mere idea of seeing the bartender again has me both wanting to run for the hills … and throw myself over the bar to be closer to any place he's stood before.

This physical reaction is going to get me in trouble if I'm not careful.

4

Vaughn

I T'S HER.

She comes out of nowhere, walking down the gritty alley in her leather jacket, arms full of books. She stopped at the sight of Aaron and me, probably surprised to see anyone at all, but then she used that alley like it was her damn runway.

I had to rip off my helmet to see her clearly. Look into those sapphire eyes again. Watch those full hips swaying with each step. Until Aaron wouldn't shut up, and I had to turn to hear what he was yammering on about. She was gone by the time I looked back.

If she's here for her credit card, I'm damn sure going to be the one to give it to her.

I leave Aaron in the alley, yelling after me, and stride through the employee entrance into the bar. I dump my helmet and jacket in the back office, wash my hands, and run my wet fingers through my hair. But just before I go through the door to the main bar, I pause.

What the hell am I doing? I've been moving purely on instinct, reacting to this indescribable physical pull, but I know literally nothing about this girl.

And, I remind myself, *dating is the last thing you can take on right now.*

Not while juggling my main job here at the bar plus all my side hustles. I don't have time for distraction if I want to pay my dad back before the end of the century.

Shaking my head, and at a much more reasonable pace, I walk out and step behind the bar.

The curvy blonde waits.

Her hair spills over her shoulders in waves, a contrast to the structured jacket that makes her look like such a badass. A blush rides high on her soft cheekbones, emphasizing the deep pink of her full lips. A stack of books is piled in front of her.

I'm a sucker for a girl who reads. I know, it's a weird kink. But I struggle to hold conversations with people I don't know well—the words never come out right. Books give common ground. Plus, who the hell doesn't like stories? Being able to read and literally not do anything else ... it's a moment of calm I don't get anywhere else. My apartment is bursting with second-hand novels and classics I saved from my college days. Having someone to talk to about books, not social media shit or celebrity gossip or whatever else people pointlessly prattle on about, would be amazing.

Our eyes meet. She gives me a shy smile, and I swear my knees almost buckle.

I'm going to make this girl mine if it's the last thing I do.

But for the moment, I just need to get it together so I don't scare her away completely.

"Welcome back," I say, coming to a stop in front of her.

Her blush deepens, and she drops my gaze. Did she not think I would remember? Maybe she didn't want me to.

"Hi," she says, looking down at the bar. I see her lips turn down for the briefest moment, and then she inhales and pulls herself up straighter. The change in posture draws my attention to her full chest, and I can't help but follow the plunge of her blouse down, down, down, until the edge of the bar stops the view. She raises her eyes again to look at me, the piercing blue driving straight into my soul like a dagger. "I left my credit card here the other night. Landon Davis."

I turn her name over in my mind.

"Give me a sec, Landon." I taste her name on my tongue. It suits her.

As I flip through the stack of forgotten cards in the cash register, a war rages in my gut. If I hand over the card, she's going to leave. Who knows if she'll ever be back? I don't know why it matters so much to me, but the fear that I won't see her again loops on repeat in my brain.

Her name pops out at me amid the other squares of plastic, and I run my calloused fingers over the raised ridges of her card, stalling.

Aaron walks out.

"Well, that was rude of you," he says to me, though he doesn't actually sound angry.

Landon's card in my hand, I shrug. "Sorry, I knew we were running late. Customer service and all that."

Aaron gives me a skeptical look before his eyes flit to Landon sitting at the bar. He rolls his muscled shoulders back, attention fixed on her, and a flare of jealousy rocks through me. I know objectively that Aaron is handsome. The ladies who come into Sullivan's fawn over him to no end. Normally, I couldn't care less, but with Landon ...

I pull myself up to my full height, about two inches taller than Aaron, and lift my chin aggressively. I don't know where this alpha possessive streak is coming from, but I can't turn it off. I step forward, making to get between Aaron and Landon, but something registers in his expression. A sly smile, of all things, splits across his face. Quick as a flash and before I can do anything to react, he uses his ex-football player instincts to dodge around me and lean against the bar before Landon.

"Hey there! What can we get ya?" he says cheerily.

I move closer, feeling irrationally annoyed. "She's just here to pick up her credit card."

"Ah, come on now!" Aaron's voice is jovial. "She can at least stay for a drink. And look at all this stuff—looks like she's here to stay for a while. That right?"

Landon shakes her head. "I'm just here for this. Thanks so much," she says as I reluctantly slide her card across the bar. "I was going to head to a coffee shop to do some work."

"You know there aren't really any coffee shops on the block, right? You gonna lug all that around with you?" Aaron asks.

"That wasn't the plan, but I ran out of gas on Rose Street—missing credit card and all that." Landon waves her credit card in the air and gives us a you-know-how-it-goes shrug. "I didn't want to leave all the stuff in my car. So, now that I've got my card, I'll walk back and see if I can pick up a gas can on the way. Maybe at some point before dark, I'll actually do some work. No guarantees, though," she says with a bright smile at Aaron.

My stomach swoops. I want that smile directed at *me.*

"And full transparency, I didn't realize there wasn't any coffee nearby ... I only moved here a few months ago," she explains. "But I'll figure it out."

My friend—the damned charming bastard—is already in planning mode. "Woah, there. On Rose? That's like, a mile off."

"Yeah, I picked a great day to wear heels," she jokes.

I know I should say something, take an active role in the conversation instead of standing here like a statue. By all accounts, she's had a shitty day so far. And she was likely stood up the other night. But here she is, bantering about it good-naturedly with Aaron, and I can't summon up even basic English.

Aaron continues, "Look, we've got coffee, and it's not bad. You're already here with all your stuff. Let me grab you a cup—on the house. Set up, do your work. It'll be quiet in here for a few hours yet."

Damn it. I should've thought of that. I mentally kick myself for being so stupid.

Landon furrows her brow, and her eyes briefly slide to mine. I can't tell if she's just being polite and trying to include me in the conversation, or if she feels the same pull as I do. "You don't need to do that," she says.

This might be my last chance. I clear my throat. "Stay. I'll get you coffee. It's my fault for letting you leave without your card the other night."

After another moment's hesitation, she nods. "Thank you. Both of you."

Evidently, Aaron isn't done yet. Leaning back and crossing his arms, he looks between Landon and me. I've seen this expression before. He's up to something.

"When you're ready to head back to your car, Vaughn can give you a ride. He just needs to stay until Javi gets here for the evening shift, but after that, he's good to head out whenever you're set to go," Aaron says.

"Oh gosh, no, I couldn't ask him to do that," Landon splutters. And, to me, "You don't have to."

I open my mouth—whether to agree or argue, I'm not even sure yet—but Aaron continues, "It'd be his pleasure. After all, we're all about customer service here! I've got a spare helmet in the back you can use. And Vaughn's been working too much lately anyway. You're really doing him a favor by helping him escape a few hours early."

The bastard is basically preening he's so pleased with himself. I don't know whether I want to punch him or hug him—or curl up under the bar and die.

"Alright, Vaughn, go get that coffee brewing. Good luck with your work … what was your name?" Aaron asks.

Landon introduces herself, and Aaron reaches out a huge hand, fully engulfing hers up to the wrist as they shake. I bristle at the sight.

"I'm Aaron, owner of this fine establishment. And this is Vaughn, my broody barkeep and resident barista." He points his thumb over his shoulder at me.

Yep, I'm definitely at the curl-up-under-the-bar-and-die stage right now.

"Hi," Landon says again, this time with a genuine smile that has me feeling heat in all sorts of distracting places.

Even though I really need to get this full work shift in, I can't *not* give her a ride now. I'd look like the biggest jerk in the world. And anyway, I don't remember ever wanting to do anything *more*. I'll just have to make up the hours another night—or make Aaron hand over a share of the tips I'm missing, having been volunteered as Sullivan's newest on-call driver.

Before I can say something stupid, I turn away to brew the coffee. Out of the corner of my eye, I see Landon open her laptop and start flicking through her notebook.

People gradually filter in over the next hour or two, but Landon doesn't seem to notice. Every time I glance her way in between making cocktails and pouring beers, she's hyperfocused on her computer screen, tapping away at the keyboard.

I desperately want to know what she's working on. I can't fathom keeping that level of focus despite all the people and distractions milling around.

Finally, I can't stand it anymore.

I grab the pot of coffee and go to give her a refill.

"So ..." I start awkwardly.

Wow, Vaughn, such a smooth-talker, I think to myself in despair.

I get it together enough to add, "What kind of work do you do?"

It takes her a moment to disconnect from what she's typing. But when her eyes finally fall on me, she seems bright and excited. "Oh, I'm a writer."

She misunderstood me. "Ah, I meant, what do you do for your job?"

Her brow furrows. "I'm a writer?"

"That's your full-time job?" I ask, confused.

"Yep, it is indeed." Some of the light in her eyes dims.

Well, I'm officially the biggest idiot in the world. I can't believe I just second-guessed her like that. "I'm so sorry, I didn't mean to imply ..." I trail off. "Honestly, I didn't realize people actually made a living writing, you know, beyond the big names. It always seems like one of those pipe dreams that can't pay the bills."

Fantastic, you dumbass. You're making it worse. Why are you bringing up whether or not she can pay her bills? I have the sense of descending deeper and deeper into my self-dug grave.

This is why I choose growling over conversation.

But I can't stop. I scramble, trying to win back the ground I've lost. "That's awesome. Really. I studied English, so ... What are you writing now? Anything interesting?"

I'm all over the place. I scrub a hand roughly over my beard. My cheeks are on fire—I can't remember the last time that happened. What is it about this woman that sends me to pieces?

Before she can answer, a shattering sound makes us both jump.

One of the old-timers in a back booth dropped his glass, and sharp shards sparkle all over the floor. I mentally swear a series of curse words that would've made my mom smack me across the back of the head had she been alive to hear them. But maybe it's a blessing in disguise that this conversation has been sidetracked. I can gather myself and try again.

"I gotta deal with that," I say. She nods. I take a final shot. "You can tell me about your writing when I come back."

Landon tilts her head, those big blue eyes holding me captive. The world spins a little.

"Okay," she replies.

The relief hits me like a tidal wave.

I need to go find the broom, but I can't resist taking a final look over my shoulder at her as I walk away. Her hands cradle her coffee cup, the glow of her computer lights her face like a halo. She sees me look, and her lips quirk up on one side in a small half-smile, revealing a single dimple.

Yeah. I'm a fucking goner.

5

LANDON

MY BREATH HITCHES AS I watch the broody bartender rake his fingers through his hair after cleaning up the broken glass.

Vaughn.

I can't figure out what his deal is, but for whatever reason, he seems interested in me. He asked to hear about my writing. *My* writing. It's probably not romantic interest, but still.

Unless he's just being nice to the girl that got stood up, the negative voice in my head whispers.

I shake it off. Because, if nothing else, my trip here has done one thing: prove Beatrice right. I didn't believe her super-sense for stories was a real thing, but something about this bar—and its bartender—absolutely shattered my writer's block. The smells of coffee, beer, leather, and wood blend together in a deep aroma. The dim light makes it easy to focus on the screen. The steady buzz of light chatter is like white noise that superpowers my brain. The relaxed and lyric-free music makes it easy for my own words to flow.

Basically, I sat down, and the words came running.

And you know what? Even if I'm not the type of woman Vaughn goes for, I can damn well write a story where I am. Which is how I've ended up with the first chapter of a romance novel that may or may not have a tattooed bartender as its hero.

I mean, I'm not the kind of girl to look an inspiration-horse in the mouth.

Plus, I'm still going all in with my main character energy. I had a momentary lapse in confidence when Vaughn first approached, but I put my big girl panties back on and went for it. And hey, I got a free coffee.

I also really like the feeling of standing with my shoulders back, acting like I'm sexy and desirable even if I don't fully feel like it. It's like inhabiting another woman's skin. It makes me feel free, unburdened by all the self-consciousness and insecurities that normally swirl through my thoughts. Who knew all I needed to do was get a mantra and shrug the negative stuff off like a bad coat?

Maya is really onto something with this.

I continue writing for a few minutes, then glance at the clock and do a double take. I can't believe how long I've been here nursing my free coffee. I need to start walking back before it gets dark.

The thought splashes cold water on my good mood. Aaron said Vaughn would give me a ride to my car, but Vaughn hadn't looked pleased with the idea. Did he ever actually agree to it?

I frown.

I'll just finish this coffee and slip out. No way do I want him feeling obligated to give me a ride when he doesn't want to.

My shoulders deflate at the thought of leaving without talking to him again. It was certainly unexpected to hear he was an English major. We could've shared our favorite books and authors ... but the last thing I'm going to do is force someone to spend time with me if they don't want to.

I'd rather be alone.

I down the last of my coffee and close my laptop. Vaughn is mixing cocktails for two young women who are clearly out for happy hour and a good time. My stomach drops when he says something that makes both women laugh out loud. I can't fathom what it could be—he's been so gruff with me.

Sighing, I gather up my stuff and slip out the door onto the street.

What started as a beautiful day has morphed into an overcast evening. Typical Pacific Northwest—the clouds don't stay away for long. It's not raining yet, but petrichor permeates the air, and the sky hangs heavy like a steel slab over my head. Thick mist blocks the top of the trees that line the street. It's only a mile back to Rose Street, and I'm pretty sure there's a gas station just a few blocks from there, but it doesn't look likely that I'll make it before the downpour starts.

The ground clacks under my heels as I stride over the uneven pavement, books and laptop held tight to my chest.

I make it about four blocks before the sprinkling rain starts.

Perfect.

A rumble rents the air.

And now there's thunder too. Awesome.

The roaring sound grows louder, and I turn. It's not thunder at all. A huge black motorcycle pulls up beside me, its rider idling the bike before pulling off his helmet.

Vaughn.

He came to find me.

"Uh, hi," I say awkwardly, squinting at him through the intensifying rain.

"How about that ride?" His voice is deep and gravelly.

Without waiting for an answer, he gets off the bike and stalks toward me. A shiver runs down my spine as he moves closer, and I tilt my chin up to meet his dark eyes. His presence wraps around me like a barrier, shielding me from the world.

I like the feeling.

A lot.

Vaughn takes the laptop and books from my arms, his gloved hand brushing against mine. Sparks race up my limbs. He tucks my things away in a large saddlebag on his bike and hands me a helmet.

"Ever been on a motorcycle?" he asks.

"Um, a few times, when I was younger. My dad used to ride."

Vaughn gets back on the bike and steadies it, his booted feet solid on the pavement and his hands gripping the handlebars. "Mount up, then," he growls.

Oh, sweet lord, give me the power to withstand this man.

Biting my lip, I put on the helmet. I place a tentative hand on his leather-clad shoulder for balance. My fingers burn where they land as I imagine the skin just beneath. I swing my leg over the seat and settle my heeled boots over the foot pegs. My cheeks burn as I wrap my arms around his waist.

Even through the padded jacket, his muscle definition is palpable.

His hands find mine, and he tugs me tighter against him until my fingers overlap in the front and my breasts push against his back. Desire pools in my stomach.

"Don't let go," he instructs, holding my hands in place for a moment longer than is strictly necessary.

At this rate, he's going to have to pry me off of him.

The engine revs and we roar down the street, rain pounding down and soaking us both. I forgot about the thrill of being on a bike, the noise and the vibrations and the smells. But this time, it's not only the motorcycle that sends adrenaline pumping through my veins. Every time Vaughn's body leans one way or the other, my own body follows, holding tight against him as we move together with the curves of the road.

He remembers to stop at the gas station without me reminding him. After we leave with a small gas can, I shout instructions over the roar of the engine. He pulls to a stop next to my old sedan far too soon. Thankfully, the rain has eased, and we both take off our helmets. Vaugh pours the gas into the tank, waving away my attempts to help.

"Thank you," I say for the dozenth time. Even though it's still sprinkling, I don't get in my car, though I do try to wipe away any makeup that might be pooling under my eyes.

He takes the helmet from my arms. "My pleasure."

Hearing the word *pleasure* in his deep, gravelly voice makes my toes curl in my boots.

I stand awkwardly, not knowing what to say. I don't want this moment to end. Logically, it doesn't make sense—I've barely spoken to this man at all. But I feel the pull like a line fastened in my gut dragging me toward him.

Something flickers in his eyes. Or maybe that's just the hopeful wishes of a girl who's been alone too long.

His stoic bearing dissolves into a concerned expression. "You're soaked."

"What do you mean? Is it raining or something?" My moment of cheek earns a genuine chuckle from him. The foreign sound sends warmth radiating through my limbs. "I would've been soaked either way. And you saved me a lot of uncomfortable walking, so thank you," I continue.

The bartender studies me. How damp and frazzled do I look right now? I don't even want to know.

He runs his hands through his hair. "Look, there's a great taco place just there. Do you want to grab a bite and get warmed up?"

I blink. "Together?"

A furrow appears between his eyebrows. "That's what I was thinking. But if you'd prefer to go alone, I can leave."

"No. I mean, yes. Let's go."

I trail him around the corner. Even though I try my best, my eyes *might* slide down to his ass just one more time. Still perfect. He leads me to a small restaurant hidden down a tiny side street. As soon as the door swings open, the smell of hot food drags a groan from me.

It smells *amazing*.

There's music playing over the speakers, but even over the hustle and bustle, I can hear Vaughn's phone ding a notification. I deflate.

What if he needs to leave? What if he has plans he forgot about?

But though his hand strays to his back pocket for a moment, he seems to change his mind halfway. He ignores it.

That simple gesture, in a world where people are constantly glued to their phones, makes my heart glow. I'm surprised everyone in the restaurant can't see it shining out of my chest like a flare.

We order our food and head to one of the few small tables. His long legs brush mine under the table as we sit.

I bite my lip, nerves fluttering like butterflies in my stomach.

Main character energy. I can do this.

"So ..." I hedge, trying to break the silence. But I don't know what else to say.

"What happened with your date the other night?" he asks abruptly.

The blush blooms across my cheeks. He wants to know about *that*. Of course. He's not interested in me. This is a pity meal.

I shift in my seat. "Well, it's a bit hard to have a date when one party decides not to come."

"He didn't show?" Vaughn's voice carries a sharp edge.

"Nope."

"His loss," he says.

"Yeah. Thanks." Needing something to do with my hands, I scrape my curling hair up into a top knot. His eyes trace down my neck, and my blush deepens.

Remember, this is just a pity dinner. Don't get ahead of yourself, Landon, I scold myself.

"Do you want to talk about it?" Vaughn asks.

I look toward the back of the restaurant, pretending to study the menu but really trying to avoid his eyes. I already had to live through being stood up. The last thing I want is to rehash it with a sexy tattooed bartender who feels sorry for me already. "Not really. It's par for the course when it comes to my dating life."

"Then those men are idiots," Vaughn growls.

I clear my throat. "Yeah, well. Thank you."

Vaughn leans forward. "I'm serious. That guy, the one who stood you up, that was the biggest mistake he's ever made. Now he never gets to see how fucking beautiful you are."

The air shifts between us.

Vaughn's eyes are dark as night, and my breath catches at the intensity of his gaze. His leg brushes mine once more under the table, and he doesn't pull away. In every place our bodies touch, electricity zings through me, my skin hypersensitive to his merest movement.

I start when the waiter arrives with our food and drinks.

My margarita glass brings much-needed coolness to my flushed skin. The tension between us is so taught it feels like a tangible force with weight and mass. I cast around for something to say, needing to break this charged thing that's building up before I get too many dirty, impossible ideas.

"You said you were an English major, right? What are your favorite books?"

Even as the question pops out, I wince. Asking about books is probably the least sexy topic possible, isn't it? That should not be my go-to when trying to impress a man way out of my league.

But then again, if this man can't answer a question about books, then there's absolutely no way this can be anything beyond a ride and some shared tacos. Yeah, I might desperately want to fall in love. I might even crave this man like nothing I've ever craved before. But some things are dealbreakers, even when it comes to brooding, tattooed hunks.

For me, books are one of them.

So, I wait.

After a beat, he finally says, "How long do you have?"

I stare at him. It's not the answer I'm expecting. He grins hesitantly at me, like he doesn't know how I'll react, and my heart skips. I can't stop the wide smile from spreading across my face.

Well, this settles it. If I don't make a move on this man, I'm going to regret it for the rest of my life.

I reply, "For you, no time limit."

My answer unlocks something in him. He's been holding a wall between us, but now, he starts to drop its battlements. His broad shoulders relax a fraction, and his brow softens. Even his hands, gripped around his beer, lose some of their tension.

We talk through two rounds of drinks and a few too many tacos. About books and English classes we've both taken and our favorite professors in college. About the books we read over and over again, the novels on our to-be-read lists, and the stories stacked on our nightstands that have never been opened. About our shared love for *Zen and the Art of Motorcycle Maintenance.*

He loves novels from the 1950s, the classics and the Beat Generation. I'm more into Regency Era reads, but I also never turn my nose up at fantasy or contemporary romance.

The longer we spend together, the warmer and more alive I feel. My skin hums in his presence. He isn't just attractive—we click into place like puzzle pieces, the conversation flowing as we share our passions and the things that bring us joy.

"So, what were you working on today? At Sullivan's?" he asks, picking at the few remaining crumbs on his plate. "Were you writing?"

Nerves flutter in my stomach, but I remember my mantra. I am Badass Author Landon now. "Actually, I was working on a novel."

"No shit. What—"

A shadow falls over us. "Um, excuse me, but are you two done?" A woman with a skirt the size of a belt stands beside our table, looking from Vaughn to me to the empty plates and cups around us.

Brought back to reality, I see that the restaurant is packed, with a huge line of people waiting for food and a table. We're taking up prime real estate.

"If not, it's okay, but it seemed like you and your friend were wrapping up," she says to Vaughn. "And sometimes, you need to be a bit aggressive when there's something you want." She gives him a flirty smile, full of thinly veiled innuendo, and then glances at me as if I'm gum stuck on the pavement.

Vaughn's look is cold, but he doesn't say anything. He turns his attention to me instead.

Even though I don't want this meal to end, it doesn't seem right to stay when so many people are waiting for seats. "Yeah, we can head out."

His lips twitch down, but he stands. Ignoring the woman completely, he waits for me to start walking and then falls into step just behind me. His hand drops to rest on my lower back, gently guiding me through the crowd to the door.

I shiver when he whispers in my ear, "Will you tell me what your book is about?"

Well, if those aren't the sexiest words I've ever heard a man speak, then my name isn't Landon Davis.

6

Vaughn

L ANDON AND I BREAK out into the street. It's a dusky evening, the sky bruised with rain clouds and oncoming night. We huddle under the restaurant's tiny overhang, watching the downpour.

I'm fuming. Things were going so damn well until that woman interrupted. I'm barely controlling the urge to steal Landon away, to wrap her up in my arms until only the two of us exist in the world.

I have to get this back on track, but I know I can't do it here, while we're sheltering from the rain and avoiding customers going in and out of the little cantina.

"Landon." Her name tastes sweet on my tongue. "See me tomorrow."

I don't say it like a question. She looks up at me through dark eyelashes.

"I have the morning off, and there's something I want you to see," I continue. A prickle of guilt nudges at my subconscious, that voice reminding me that I don't have the bandwidth to date anyone for real, but I can't stop myself. The *want* overpowers my good sense.

"What is it?" Her voice sounds curious and bright, music to my ears.

"You'll have to come and see." My own voice turns deep ... and a little suggestive.

One of her eyebrows quirks up, and she smiles, showing off that adorable dimple again. "Then I guess I'll be seeing you in the morning."

We make plans for me to pick her up at her apartment before turning to look at the continuing heavy rain.

"You're going to get soaked again," I say apologetically. I wish I had a way to protect her. From the elements, from bad dates, from broken-down cars, from the world.

"Yeah ... there's really only one way to handle this," she replies with a serious nod. And with no hesitation, she runs straight out into the rain. She laughs as the cold water hits her. She turns to look back at me, grinning wide. "Come on!"

I go after her, watching her glorious curvy figure as she jogs toward her car. While she ducks into her sedan, still laughing, I grab her things from the saddlebag of my

Harley. After passing them through the window to her, I shake the rain from my hair and lean down close.

"Thank you again. For today," she says.

"Of course."

"I'll see you tomorrow."

"Fuck yeah, you will," I growl. Her breath hitches at my tone, and desire flares in my gut. It takes every ounce of willpower to stand and walk back to my bike. Tomorrow can't come soon enough.

I spend all night tossing and turning, going back and forth between excitement and guilt about asking Landon out. I know I can't take on a real relationship. There's no point when I work constantly and have this loan hanging over my head like a noose. That voice inside keeps nagging at me, telling me that I'm making a huge mistake, that I need to stay focused ... but I'm so damn tired of listening to it.

I can't help but think Landon and I could be something real. Despite the loan, despite my dad, despite everything. Maybe I can actually open up to her.

A realization falls over me. That all those things I felt in law school—not wanting to go out, not wanting to engage, not wanting to *do* anything—are pretty damn similar to how I've been feeling lately.

Miserable. Lonely. Exhausted. Closed off to the world. Sinking deeper and deeper into myself.

Until last night, that is, when some of the load finally seemed to lift. It was like a breath of fresh air after being underwater for a few seconds too long. Painful and invigorating, all at once.

Of course, Landon can't become the sole source and controller of my well-being. I'm responsible for how I'm feeling, regardless of whether she's around. But something about spending time with her just reminded me, I guess, of what it feels like to really *live*.

After a night spent pondering such deep things, I arrive at Landon's in the morning as a bundle of nerves. I can't wait a second longer to see her, but I'm terrified it won't feel the same.

I steel myself before knocking, trying to play it cool.

When she answers the door, all my stress melts away.

She's in a sweater that reveals the smooth curve of her collarbone and shoulder on one side. My eyes track hungrily across her creamy skin. My gaze falls to the tight black jeans and boots that rise halfway up her thick, gorgeous thighs. I clear my throat, suddenly struggling to get enough air.

"Hi," she says. She smiles shyly.

"Nice boots," I reply, more growl than words.

"Thanks. I like nice things." She gives me a wink, and I melt a little.

But as her words sink in, a twinge of concern flashes through me. I can't give her nice things. I can't take care of her financially. Will that be a dealbreaker for her?

Woah, Vaughn, you're getting ahead of yourself. Just see how today goes first.

I brush aside the negative thoughts. As we leave her place, I take a risk and interlace my fingers with hers. Her piercing blue eyes shoot me a look, but her hand relaxes into mine. It feels like rose petals against my calloused skin.

"Your Harley's beautiful," she says as we approach my bike. "I'm super excited to ride again today."

The fact that she notices my bike and wants to ride again sends pleasure swooping through me. "Thank you," I grind out, once I remember how to speak. "It's taken a lot of work to get her here." Hours and hours and hours of work, searching for parts, treating the leather, upgrading different pieces to be just how I want them.

"You did it yourself?" she asks.

"Yeah."

"That's some serious dedication, to learn enough to do all the work yourself. And to put the time in, too. I'm impressed." She smiles up at me.

It's a damn miracle I don't kiss her then and there. Not only because she's gorgeous and enjoys reading and likes my Harley, but because she recognizes the effort I put into something I care so much about.

When she climbs up behind me on the bike, with those booted legs within such easy reach, I nearly implode. My phone starts to ring, but I silence it without looking at the caller ID. I have much better things to worry about.

Thankfully, the roar of the engine and the smooth ride take the edge off my sky-high emotions. I'm still hyperaware of Landon—but in the best way possible. As we ride out of the town center and up into the mountains, I hear her squealing with excitement at the beautiful views that pop in and out of sight.

Landon has only been here a few months, so I'm going to take advantage of her newness and show her one of the best hidden spots around here.

We pull into the parking lot. Even though I've been to the Cliff Haven Café dozens of times, I still feel the same sense of awe as we walk inside. It's nestled high in the mountains, and the far wall of the restaurant is all windows. Diners look out over miles of emerald-green forest and rugged mountain peaks. The main feature of the landscape, though, is the giant waterfall thundering down in the near distance.

Landon's mouth hangs open as she stares. "I've never seen anything like this," she whispers. Then she looks at me. "And it smells so good. So, so good."

It's true. In addition to having the best view in the country, this place has the best breakfast in town. They make all their own pastries in-house, and the whole café is filled with the sweet aroma of baked goods. It explains why, even though it's a ways out of town and early on a Sunday morning, it's already crowded with people.

"Just wait. It's gonna blow your mind."

"I'm literally already drooling," she says happily. "Hang on, I need to get a better look at this."

Landon weaves through the patrons until she's standing right in front of the window with a clear view of the waterfall. And I'm treated to my own glorious view of her ample ass in those tight jeans. My phone dings in my pocket, but it sounds far, far away. I clear my throat and go instead to the counter, buying myself time to drag my mind out of the gutter.

I've got another surprise in store for her.

I give the host my name, and he returns a moment later with a giant brown bag. I called ahead this morning to make sure our food would be ready to go, just in case there was a morning rush. And even though the interior of the restaurant is fantastic, I want to show her something a little different. Thankfully, it's a mild morning, and the sun peaks out from behind lazily floating clouds.

Landon walks back over to me, eyeing the bag. "Aren't we staying?"

"I've got something else in mind. Follow me."

She looks skeptical when we go back outside into the parking lot. But I just smile at her furrowed brow and take the lead, ducking around the corner of the restaurant onto a little dirt trail.

"You're not going to murder me, are you?" she says from behind me.

I turn and see her picking her way carefully down the hill in those sexy boots. The path is a bit slick after last night's rain. God, I really should've told her to wear something more comfortable. Or less expensive, given how fancy they look.

But at the same time, I'm selfishly glad I didn't. She drools at the aroma of freshly baked pastries—I drool at the sight of her in those boots.

"Don't you trust me?"

I reach out a hand and grasp hers, steadying her as she comes up next to me.

"I suppose I do," she replies. My chest can't possibly hold all my roiling emotions. She trusts me. And I feel like a fucking king for it.

"It's not far. I promise."

Landon nods, and I start walking again, still holding her hand.

We haven't gone more than a few steps when she slips. I feel it more than see it, and before I can consciously process what I'm doing, I drop the food and rotate my body to grab her. My arms wrap around her in a bear hug.

She cries out in fear as we drop.

I don't make it in time to stop her fall entirely, but I do manage to get part of my body behind hers so I hit the ground first, taking the brunt of the impact. But she still lands partially on the rocky trail.

My emotions go into overdrive. I prop myself up, still cradling her in one arm, and frantically look over her body for visible injuries.

"Are you okay? Are you hurt?"

Landon is pale and breathing hard, but she nods. "I'm okay."

"Are you sure?" Fear grips my throat like a vice. When she doesn't answer immediately, I say the words more forcefully. "Landon, are you sure?"

She takes a deep breath. "Yeah, I'm okay. That just scared the crap out of me."

Her eyes meet mine, and I realize how close we are. I'm almost on top of her, lying in the dirt.

"You sure you're alright?" I can't stop myself from asking again, if only to keep her here for a moment longer.

"Yes, I'm sure. Thank you for saving me. Shall we ... get up now?" A teasing smile spreads slowly across her face.

I'm still breathing a bit harder than normal, but I pull us both to our feet. I don't let go yet, though. Her chest visibly rises and falls as she clutches my arms, still regaining her sense of footing.

"I'm sorry. I should have told you to wear different shoes," I say. The guilt rips through me. If she'd been injured, it would've been all my fault.

"And I would have worn these anyway," she says, still grinning. But as she studies my face, her expression grows more serious. "It's not your fault I slipped, Vaughn. Sometimes unlucky things just happen, and we fall on our asses. And that's okay. *I'm* okay," she emphasizes.

I exhale slowly, trying to calm my racing heart. I feel her grip tighten on my forearm for a brief moment, and it pulls me back into myself.

Suddenly, I'm hyperaware of my hands resting on her hips. Of her body pressed close against mine. Of our breath mixing in the crisp morning air. Of how secluded we are here on this path in the woods. Of the space between us that could be so easily crossed if only I would just ... lean.

I slide my hands up, ever so slowly. But as soon as my fingers find her waist, she flinches, takes a half step back, and puts her hands between us, not quite pushing me away but making it clear that she's uncomfortable.

I immediately drop my hands. I don't know what I did wrong, but whatever moment there was between us breaks.

Landon gives a shaky sigh. "I'm sorry. I just ... I don't like having my stomach touched." She starts brushing the lingering dirt off her clothes, avoiding my eyes.

I frown. "Why don't you like being touched?"

"I didn't say I don't like being touched. I just don't like when someone feels this." She motions to her stomach with both hands. "It's embarrassing."

Now I'm really confused. "Embarrassing?"

She lets out an exasperated noise. "Yes. When you're told your whole life that fat is bad, that to be in a bigger body is shameful, that stomachs should show abs and ribs, not rolls, it's hard not to feel self-conscious when someone touches your body."

It feels like someone just hit me in the face. It's never occurred to me, not once, that she might feel this way. "Who told you that?"

Landon's quiet laugh is sad. "Everyone. My parents, other women, other men, magazines, TV, social media. Every personal trainer who's automatically assumed I'm at the gym to lose weight. Every set of uncomfortable shapewear designed to mold my body into an 'acceptable' form. Ever wondered why you don't see bodies like mine in lingerie ads or as the leads in movies? This world sees bigger bodies as less beautiful, less healthy, less sexy, less worthy. It's hard to break out of that thinking when it's reinforced everywhere you look," she finishes in a whisper, her cheeks flaming red.

I may not be able to fix this fucked-up world that made Landon feel less than, but I can certainly try to fix this. "Landon, you're fucking gorgeous. You know that, right?"

She only looks at her feet.

"I don't give a damn what you've heard from anyone else. I told you last night, I'm telling you now, and I'll tell you every day if I have to. Your curves … believe me. Men would kill over those curves. Your body isn't shameful, and it's not something you should ever be embarrassed of. It's a fucking *triumph*."

A long silence lingers between us. I let the words hang in the air, hoping she hears them.

"Thank you, but can we change the subject, please? Thank you for catching me, just now. It was a lot nicer falling into your arms than onto the ground."

Those blue eyes are still downcast, and I see the flush creeping across her chest now. I almost press the issue, wanting to convince her of just how incredible she is, how beautiful every inch of her luscious body is, but I can tell she's not comfortable having the conversation. And I'm not good with this kind of thing, the feelings and emotions and subtleties. I usually just make everything worse. So, I let it drop. For now.

"Anytime." I rake my fingers through my hair, pushing it out of my face. I see the fallen bag on the edge of the path. "Though I might've ruined breakfast."

"I'm sure it will still taste great." Now that we've moved onto a new topic, Landon seems to be falling back into her normal cheery self again. She picks up the bag of food. "Lead on, Superman."

I must admit, I like my new nickname.

7

LANDON

V AUGHN AND I MAKE our way down the little hiking trail, him in the lead. I can't stop my mind from swirling over what I just said. I'm horrified I pointed out my stomach fat ... and went on a mini-rant about systemic fatphobia and all my insecurities.

And that was after I fell on my ass and brought him down with me.

Part of me wants to hide behind one of these trees and pretend I'm invisible. But when I remember him calling me gorgeous, calling me a *triumph*, I step even closer.

He's too perfect. He's like a cinnamon roll, sweet and nice and earnest and a bit shy, all wrapped up in a badass, brooding, and tattooed exterior. He says all the right things, too. I want to believe them so badly—and when he says them, part of me does.

Then there are those moments between us when it's like electricity sparking in the air.

Vaughn looks over his shoulder at me. His eyes travel down my body to my boots before making their way back up to my face. His eyes are dark and molten, even in the clear sunlight. It makes me feel a certain sort of way, deep in the pit of my stomach.

This can't be my imagination. This is something real. And I'm not going to let my lack of confidence talk me out of something that could be life-changing.

So I let the insecurities fall, imagining each of them dropping over the side of the tall ravine into the waterfall. I visualize pulling back on my main character energy like a fabulous coat. I stand tall. I'm ready for whatever comes next.

Or at least, I think I am.

A moment later, we emerge from a thick patch of trees and into a world from a fairytale.

We stand on a small outcrop of land with a single bench perched upon it, looking out over the roaring waterfall. We're near the top of the falls, and I peek over the edge and see a massive pool of foaming water below us, several stories down. Jagged, snow-capped mountain peaks are etched against the horizon in the distance.

Tiny pinpricks of cold water form a mist in the air, and when I taste ice, I realize my mouth is hanging open in awe. I suck in a breath.

Vaughn sits on the bench and pats the space beside him. "You can't live in Temptation Falls without seeing the town's namesake. And I thought you might like breakfast with a view."

"You thought right," I breathe, turning once more to see the waterfall. After a long look, I walk over to him. "Thank you. This is spectacular. I thought the restaurant was amazing, but this?" I motion around me, at a loss for words. "It's like magic. I've never seen anything so beautiful in my life."

"Neither have I," he replies, but he's not looking at the waterfall. He's looking at me. My blood heats.

I sit beside him, heaving the bag of food into the space between us. I unfurl the folded top of the bag and sigh dreamily. This is what paradise must smell like: freshly baked pastry, pine trees, and ... a small hint of soap and leather from the man seated next to me.

The food is a little squished from when Vaughn dropped the bag, but it's literally the best croissant I've ever eaten in my life.

"How do you know about this place?" I ask, wiping crumbs from my mouth.

"I grew up coming here with my mom. We would eat these giant breakfasts before hiking the trails. She used to say the walks were to shake the food from her stomach to her toes." Vaughn smiles at the memory. "God, I haven't thought about that in ages."

"Are you close with your mom?"

"I was," he says.

"Not anymore?"

"She died about ten years ago."

"Oh, Vaughn, I'm so sorry. I didn't realize. What about your dad?"

His back goes rigid, and he looks away from me. "We're not close." His voice is sharp and laced with something dark. He glances down at his watch.

"I'm sorry." It comes out as a whisper. I'm not sure if I'm sorry about his mom, sorry he's not close with his dad, or sorry about asking the wrong question. Maybe all of them.

"It's okay. It was a long time ago." He glances at me, and his rugged, handsome face softens, the creases falling away as we hold eye contact. "Really, it's okay. Are you close with your family?"

I seize the chance at a subject change.

"Yeah, I am, but we're all a bit scattered now. My parents moved to Arizona a couple years ago. They love the heat and sunshine. Then there's my brother, who is basically a vagabond."

"What do you mean, he's a vagabond?" Vaughn asks. An incredulous smile spreads over his face, and the rush of pleasure that comes with the sight melts away all the remaining tension.

"I don't know how else to describe it!" I laugh. "He's constantly bouncing from place to place. One year it's van life, one year it's backpacking through Europe. He's in New Zealand right now working on a farm. I keep hoping he'll settle down so I can actually spend some time with him. But for now, he's living his best life. He's incredible. He literally never worries about anything, just goes where the wind takes him. And it all seems to work out for him."

"I'm jealous." There's that dark edge to his voice again. But he continues, "So, it's you and your brother?"

"And my sister. She's in London for a job right now. She works in fashion, and she's styling all these incredible celebrities in between jet-setting around Europe in her stilettos. This is the longest I've gone without seeing her in person ... we're only a year apart, so we've always been really close. Having her so far away sucks, but I'm happy she's chasing her dreams."

"And you? Are you chasing your dreams?" Vaughn asks.

I think for a moment, studying his sharp profile as he looks out at the waterfall. He glances down at his watch again, and it's like ice in my stomach. Am I boring him? Does he not want to hear any of this? Maybe he doesn't want to be here after all.

I shake off the thought.

"I'm trying. That's what brought me here, I guess. The dream of a small town in a beautiful place where I can start fresh. Plus, something about the idea of the rain and the gorgeous views spoke to the romantic writer in me—I love curling up by a fire with a soft blanket and a book, and this seemed like a good place for it."

"What do you think so far?" He sounds a little hesitant. When he turns to look at me, a small crease appears between his eyebrows.

I gesture around us. "Look at this place! It's incredible! I mean, yeah, moving to a new place alone is challenging. It's been lonely and a bit overwhelming. But then I have experiences like this, and everything is worth it. There are these moments when everything feels like it's finally falling into place. Do you ever get that feeling?"

As soon as I stop talking, I feel like I've said too much. Asked too personal of a question. Vaughn's face is serious, and he scrubs his hand over his beard a few times. But he replies, "Yeah, once in a while, I do."

He holds my gaze, and a shiver crawls up my spine.

"Thank you again for bringing me here," I say softly.

He nods. We sit together, sometimes talking and sometimes sitting comfortably in silence, staring out at the forest and the waterfall. The sun goes behind a cloud, and I shiver again, this time with the chill. He stretches one long arm out and wraps it over my shoulder, tucking me protectively into his side. Maybe I'm just imagining it, but

I swear I fit perfectly into the space. He smells like man and leather, and it's intoxicating.

After a moment, the hand resting over my shoulder begins to move. His fingers lightly trace up and down my upper arm. I'm frozen, pinned in place by the goosebumps radiating out from every place he touches. When his thumb massages that sore point between my neck and shoulder, I almost moan. And his broad fingers dancing along my collarbone and then back down my arm? They promise all sorts of delicious things.

What else can these hands do?

I never would have thought this was a turn-on of mine, but I'm learning all sorts of things about myself with this man.

I tilt my head, leaning it against his broad shoulder, which also has the added benefit of giving his hand better access to my neck. He growls his approval and pulls me tighter against him.

Vaughn is just beginning some fresh, exquisite exploration when he looks at his watch and curses. He straightens and lets me go.

"Shit. I'm so sorry, but we need to get going," he says.

The spell breaks, leaving me bereft without his touch.

He stands and looks down at me, eyes soft. "I've got a shift at the bar," he says. "Otherwise, I'd stay here all damn day. But unfortunately, my day off isn't until tomorrow."

My insides warm. So that's why he was checking his watch so much. He reaches out a hand and helps me to my feet. He towers above me, even in my heels, and I fight the urge to simply fall and let him catch me once more.

We head back up the path.

"So," he prods after a moment of silence. "Tell me about your book."

He remembers.

I hesitate, looking down at the trail as if we're in a particularly tricky section—which we're not. "It's kind of embarrassing," I say.

Genuine confusion furrows his brow. "What are you talking about? You're writing a book, how could that be embarrassing?"

"Let's just say, it's not the next Great American Novel."

"And?" He takes my hand and gives it an encouraging squeeze.

Should I tell him? Will he judge me?

Maya's words float back to the surface. *If you were the main character in your story, if you were the badass protagonist—or the badass author I know you want to be—what would you do?*

I know the answer. Badass Author Landon would take a shot, potential embarrassment be damned.

"I'm writing a romance novel, actually," I say.

"Oh yeah?"

"Yeah. I'm not very far, to be honest, but I got in the groove yesterday." A beat passes. "I had good inspiration."

My stomach swoops with nervous energy. I can't believe I just said that.

We emerge back out into the parking lot and stop at his bike, neither of us making a move to grab our helmets.

"What happens in your romance novel?" Vaughn's voice has dropped an octave in the last ten seconds.

I gather my courage and look up into his magnetic eyes. He's staring at me through those thick black lashes with an intensity that sends goosebumps up my arms. Dark waves cascade over his brow, and it takes everything in me not to reach up and comb them back with my fingers. His phone dings, but he doesn't make a move to check it.

Main character energy. Here we go.

"Well, it's set in a bar. And the hero is a broody bartender."

8

VAUGHN

Does she mean what I think she means?

After breakfast, after this time with her, I already feel like a new man. Like a weight has lifted off my shoulders. I didn't think it could get any better, but now? If she's saying what I think she's saying …

I swear this woman was designed just for me. To bring me out of the dark place I've been living in, alone and lonely.

I growl, "Broody, huh?"

Her lips twist to the side in a shy smile, and that dimple peeks out. "Yep. Very much so."

I want to taste those lips, to kiss the word *broody* right out of her vocabulary. My phone starts to ring, and I silence it immediately.

I gaze down at her, at the blush blooming across her cheeks, the tendrils of hair curling around her face. This woman is *mine.* The possessive feeling lights a fire in my chest. I lean closer, my breath catching when she tilts her chin up a fraction in response to my movement.

Landon continues, her voice smoky, "But, you know, it would really help if I could do some real-world research. Kinda like when a crime writer goes on a ride-along with a cop. Maybe I need to do another day with a bartender." Her voice drops to a whisper. "Or maybe a night."

Our faces are only an inch apart now.

She goes on, "Find out what it's really like to—"

My lips find hers before she can finish her sentence. I kiss her softly, gently, wanting to savor it like aged scotch. My hands lift to cup her face, and after a moment, she melts into me with a quiet moan. Fireworks explode in my chest.

I don't care if we're in the middle of a crowded parking lot and everyone in the restaurant can see us. I want them to see. Let them see that this goddess has chosen *me.*

Someone catcalls us, whooping like an asshole, but I don't give a damn about that either. I simply turn us slightly, putting my back to the restaurant and using my own body to shield Landon from view.

My hands slide down her body to skim over the outer curve of her breasts, just like I've been dreaming about. She doesn't stop me when my fingers find her waist, but I drop them down to her hips instead, not wanting to make her feel uncomfortable when everything else is so damn perfect.

But I've only just begun everything I intend to do when my phone rings once more, the sound like a siren, ripping our moment of closeness into pieces.

Who the hell can't get the hint?

Landon pulls back, her breathing a little ragged. "You should probably get that. It might be important."

I growl. That seems to be my go-to around her.

Reluctantly, I drop my hands and pull my phone from my back pocket. The incoming call cuts off right as I look down and see my dad's name. My home screen reveals a series of missed texts and calls. That's unusual, even for the perpetual nag that is my father.

Almost immediately, the phone begins to ring again.

"Can you give me a minute?" I ask.

"Of course." Landon puts a hand on my Harley as if to steady herself, and satisfaction roars through me that I'm able to make this woman swoon. My eyes travel over those tight jeans hugging every inch of her curves. Over her full, reddened lips, now forming a small frown, like she's worried about me. When was the last time someone worried about me?

It takes a Herculean effort, but I walk a few steps away and answer the phone.

"Yeah?" I say, my voice curt.

"Change of plans, Vaughn," Dad replies.

Hearing him say my name in that knife-edged voice sends ice through my veins. Normally, my father avoids any sign of recognition or familiarity, avoiding greetings and names at all costs.

"What are you talking about?" I bite out.

"It's time to pay up. I can't wait any longer on you."

"I told you," I say in a flat voice, "I'll have your payment on time this week. As usual."

My father's voice is hard steel. "You misunderstand me. I need you to pay *in full*."

"Are you fucking kidding me?" My stomach drops to the ground.

"It's been three years. I think I've given you more than enough time to figure your shit out. Now, I need that money back. I have another ... interested party whose investment is more important."

"So, you owe money to someone else, is that it? What was it, a bad bet? I thought you were done with that shit."

"It's none of your damn business, is what it is. I have been more than fair with you, and you still haven't figured your life out. I'm done waiting. I need the rest by Friday."

I grip my phone so hard the screen is in danger of shattering. "That's ten grand. How the hell am I supposed to get that in a week?" I nearly shout.

"That's on you. Just get me the money or both of us are going to have problems. That interested party I mentioned doesn't like to wait for their due. And if you don't pay up to me, your name might need to get dropped into the mix."

He's joking, right? He must be. Or is my own father seriously threatening to send whatever low-life loan shark he wronged in my direction? I can't fathom a parent doing that to their own child. Anger flares through me, the strength of which would've scared me if I wasn't so ready to crush a car with my bare hands.

I try to steady my voice, to remove all traces of emotion from it, but I can't veil my fury.

"You'll get your money, and then we're done. Do you hear me? I'm fucking done. Don't contact me. Don't call me. Don't come near the bar. Have a nice life, Dad."

I end the call and barely stop myself from throwing my phone into the wall of the café. My chest constricts, squeezing out all oxygen. I can't breathe.

The soft voice comes from behind me. "Vaughn, are you alright?"

I spin on my heel and see Landon standing a couple of paces away. Her face looks pale, and she worries her lip with her teeth. Lips still swollen from my kiss. She steps forward and lays a hand on my arm, giving it a gentle squeeze.

"What can I do to help? Whatever it is, we'll figure it out."

I close my eyes and shake my head. My breath shudders, an ice pick in my lungs.

I can't remember ever wanting someone like I want Landon. Not just physically, but all of it. And here she is, offering to help me without even knowing what's wrong. But the sad realization settles into my bones like a lead weight dragging me down.

I can't be involved in something like this right now. Especially not now, after that phone call.

If my dad does drop my name into the mix with this mysterious "interested party," anyone associated with me could be at risk. I know the guys at Sullivan's can take care of themselves, but this girl? I can't do that to her. I can't bring her into this drama and my fucked-up life. Even if I manage to pay my dad the rest of the loan by Friday, I'll be left with nothing to my name.

Whatever woman is in my life—especially *this* woman—deserves to be cared for, not to be constantly stressed that I might not be able to pay the rent … or that thugs might come after me with a baseball bat. Because honestly, I wouldn't put it past my dad at this point.

I'll never let any woman I care about feel how my mom felt in her relationship with him.

Even if I try to continue whatever this thing between us is, there's no way she'll be able to see me as a whole person, a real man, when everything in my life is in shards. She already said she likes nice things—but she can't get them with me.

I can't believe I let it go this far in the first place. Can't believe I thought I could have something for myself. I should've known it was too good to be true.

So I do what I have to do. I pull the walls I only just started letting down firmly back into place, building the fortress around my heart. It's better this way. Better to stop this now before it goes too far and we both get hurt. I need to refocus, figure out what the hell I'm going to do now.

I scrub at my beard. "Look, you're great. But I can't do this."

The sight of her face crumpling is almost enough to make me forget it all and kiss her pain away. But I can't. It isn't fair to her.

"What? What are you talking about?"

The knot in my windpipe threatens to cut off all speech, but I grind out, "This just won't work for me. I'm sorry."

"I thought …" Landon trails off, clears her throat. "If there's something going on, let me help you. You don't have to do this on your own. I'm right here."

"I don't need help. This just isn't going to work between us." My jaw works. I need to apologize, to say I'm sorry for leading her on, but I can't. I'm not sorry I got to spend this time with her. And while I *am* sorry about how I'm handling the situation, I don't know what else to do.

"I don't understand, Vaughn. What the hell just happened? Is this about your phone call? Or is this … is this about me?" Her final words are so small and quiet I can barely hear them.

I can't leave the door open. "I just can't be with you, not like this."

Her cheeks flush dark crimson. "I'm sorry, I must have misread things. Um, can you please give me a ride home now?" she whispers. She wraps her arms around her chest like they're holding her heart in place too.

Guilt lances through me. She didn't misread things at all, but there's no point in correcting her. It would only make things harder. Whatever is between us is like fire. If there's any oxygen, it's going to find a way to burn. I can't risk it.

So, asshole that I am, I just nod and say, "Yeah, let's go."

Landon stares at me for another long moment. Tears well up over those beautiful blue eyes, and the spike of pain in my gut makes me wince.

So, coward that I am, I pull my helmet on and pass over hers.

It's agony driving her home. Her arms wrap around me, but I know all she wants to do is escape this bike. Escape me. And I don't blame her.

When I finally drop her at her apartment, I wait only long enough for her to get safely on the sidewalk before I ride away without another look.

The guilt is like claws ripping my chest open.

9

LANDON

I SHUFFLE TO MY door, my coziest gray sweater wrapped tight around my body and my eyes still puffy. I swing it open.

Maya, the beautiful brunette from my writer's group, stands with a brown bag in one hand and a pizza box in the other.

"I've got white, red, and rosé. I wasn't sure what you preferred, so you get to take your pick. And of course, I brought the good carbs." Without waiting for a reply, Maya sashays in, gives me a kiss on the cheek, and sets the goods on the kitchen island.

"You are officially my favorite person in the entire world," I say gratefully. The smell of pizza is like a comforting blanket, and I inhale the cheesy goodness.

"Well, I can't say it's entirely unselfish. I'm indulging too. Now, come on, grab some plates and let's chat," she says with a smile.

After we both pour a glass of wine and get a slice of pizza, we move to my overstuffed couch.

"So, tell me what's up."

After a steadying breath, I tell Maya everything. About sitting at the bar and writing yesterday, about Vaughn coming to get me on his bike in the rain, about our conversation. About our adventure today. About the kiss. And about how it ended with that phone call. All I heard was something about owing money, and then everything fell apart.

"And I know we haven't ever hung out before like this, but I really needed someone to talk to. You were so kind the other day at writing group. I keep replaying your words about main character energy, and, well, thank you. Thank you for letting me get this all out. But I thought this guy … I know it's only been, like, two days, but I thought he might be the one," I blurt. Horrified, I blot away the tears threatening to spill over once more.

"Girl, stop that! You don't need to thank me. We're friends, okay? Us ladies gotta stick together when the men are being idiots." She brushes a strand of her long chocolate-brown hair behind her ear with a manicured finger. "Now, I think there's something we need to unpack here."

"Yes! What the hell was that phone call? Why did he ice over like that?" I say desperately. "Unless it was because of me. Because of the kiss. Some random guy catcalled us—maybe he's embarrassed by me. He said he can't be with me like this ... maybe he meant he can't be with me romantically. That he's just not into me that way. I knew he was out of my league." The tears flood back.

"Actually, that's not what needs to be unpacked. But I need you to stop that negative self-talk right now. I can guarantee that *no man* is out of your league. That's just patriarchal nonsense that puts too much value on a woman's external appearance and not enough value on, well, her values and personality. But that's something for another day," Maya huffs. She takes another bite of pizza, swallows, and continues, "Anyway, something weird clearly happened on that phone call. Honestly, though, that's the simple part. If you like this guy, and you think there's potential for a future, then you need to take another shot."

"You call that simple? That's so embarrassing!"

"It's the simplest thing in the world! You take a shot at love. If it goes well, beautiful. You live happily ever after. If he's not into you in that way, it'll be a bummer for a bit, but it's ultimately okay. You're still just as much of a catch as you were before. It has no bearing on your worth—that's what you need to remember. That's all on him. If it doesn't happen, it wasn't meant to be."

"But what about how it all fell apart at the end? What if it all goes wrong again?"

"Then it goes wrong again, but at least you took the shot. And what if it goes right? Won't it all be worth it?" She picks a piece of pepperoni off her pizza and pops it in her mouth, careful not to smudge her perfect lip gloss.

I pull my legs up underneath me on the couch and take another sip of my wine. There's some logic to that. If it doesn't go well, that's not on me.

And despite what Vaughn said about not being able to be with me, something in me still shouts that it was all real. After all, why else would he have done all those things to make sure I could see it?

Coming to find me in the rain. Calling me gorgeous on more than one occasion. Bringing me out to the waterfall today. Taking my hand as we walked, and catching me as I fell. Kissing me like *that* in the parking lot. Tracing his eyes down my body, my curves, like he wanted to devour me.

I know in my gut—even after everything—that he appreciates every inch. And it goes so much deeper than that. We truly, intimately, connect. There's no way that's fake. I know it in my bones.

But maybe that's not enough for him.

Then I remember something Maya just said. "Wait … if the Vaughn thing isn't what needs to be unpacked, what were you talking about?"

Maya grins. "Your writing! You said it yourself, you were on a roll! You kicked off that new romance novel, and the words poured right out of you. That's the kind of writing mojo we need to lean into."

"Oh, no, I can't."

The other woman narrows her brown eyes. "What are you talking about?"

"I can't keep writing that! I was writing about *him*. He inspired the whole damn thing," I say, dejected once more. "I literally had the hero standing five feet away from me. As of this morning, he wants nothing to do with me. How am I supposed to keep writing it now?"

I narrowly avoid the pillow Maya flings at my head.

"Hey!" I protest.

"You keep writing because ... You. Are. An. Author." Maya punctuates every word with a pause. "You are a *badass* author. You take your inspiration, and you use your skills to craft it into a story. That's what we do. Authors don't let other authors give up a whole book just because their date acts like a dick. Can you imagine Stephen King or Brandon Sanderson or Mark Dawson just *giving up* because a girl doesn't like them? No!"

Maya grabs another pillow, and I hurriedly raise my hands to block it. But she just clutches it tight to her stomach.

"Okay, I hear you—" I begin, but she cuts me off.

"Women sell themselves short enough. We can't let men convince us to sell ourselves even shorter. If we're going to be friends, then we're going to lift each other up. We're going to see our own worth. We're going to push each other when we need pushing, and love each other when we need loving. And we are *not* going to stop chasing our dreams because the actions of others throw us off our game for a minute. Deal?"

I can only stare and nod. Who is this magnificent creature I invited into my home?

"Sorry, I'll step off my soapbox now," Maya finishes with a sideways smile.

"Don't you dare apologize for that amazingness. I love it. All of it. And you're so freaking right. I'm not letting this stop me from finally finishing a book. I keep saying that's what I want to do, so I'm going to do it." My heart swells with excitement.

I stand, go to the kitchen, and grab the pizza box. Holding the one remaining slice before me as if it were a prized possession on a silver platter, rather than a greasy piece of pizza on a napkin, I solemnly walk back over to my friend and place it on her plate with a small bow.

"For that, you deserve the last of the carbs."

"Oh, hell yeah I do." Maya bites into it with a sigh of pleasure. After she swallows, she says, "Now, you need to go back to the bar and write your book."

I don't tell Maya this part, but the only reason I'm able to play hooky on Monday and get up the nerve to go to Sullivan's Place again is because I know Vaughn has the day off and won't be there. That doesn't make me a wimp, does it?

I just haven't decided what to do yet.

As I walk through the now-familiar doors shortly after the bar opens for the day, I'm relieved that the pressure is off.

Eyes still adjusting to the dim light, I head to the bar and take the same seat as before. No use breaking the writing mojo. The rest of the place is empty aside from a couple of old men playing cards at one table and a family at another. Two young girls, no older than twelve, face in my direction, the parents facing away.

Are kids allowed in bars these days? Maybe it's okay because it's so early.

An unfamiliar man emerges from the back room, and I can't help forgetting all about the kids to stare for a moment.

Okay, what is with this place? Is everyone *attractive?*

The man's black hair brushes the top of his white collar, and stubble grazes a sharp jawline. The dark tailored vest slung over his crisp shirt makes him look like he belongs in a men's fashion catalog. His light hazel eyes, vibrant against his olive complexion, fall on me. He gives a friendly grin and walks over.

"What can I get you?" His words pitch and tilt with a slight accent.

"Do you have coffee?" I ask.

"I haven't made the pot yet, but give me a few minutes. I can brew it up now," he says.

"That's great, thank you."

He nods with another smile and strides away.

I open my laptop and skim through what I wrote yesterday. I know this is a new genre for me, and I don't have much experience in the romance department, but honestly—my first draft is *good*. The more I read, the more excitement flutters in my chest. It feels freaking amazing. I don't need things to be working with Vaughn to make this part of my life work.

I am a badass author. I am my own main character. Hell yes.

The thought gives me a surge of confidence, and before I can change my mind, I grab my phone and type a text. I hit send. Then I send a quick follow-up.

And then I have a minor freak-out.

I stare at the delivered messages.

Oh my God, oh my God. Why the hell did I just do that? Do I sound totally nuts? Oh my GOD.

I take a deep breath in through my nose and breathe out slowly.

Well, nothing to be done about it now. If he doesn't respond, though, I might never be bold enough to show my face in this bar again … so I need to take advantage of the time I do have.

Slipping back in where I left off, I start to type.

A few minutes later, the bartender comes out and slides my coffee across the bar. Our fingers brush as I take the handle. Normally, that would make me blush. But today, it's nothing but a passing trifle. As attractive as he is, there's no spark of anything between us. Not like I have with Vaughn.

After a solid block of writing, I stretch before making my way to the ladies' room at the back of the bar. As I wash my hands, a stunning woman enters. Tall and statuesque, with platinum hair and ice-blue eyes framed with dark lashes. She smiles and stands beside me at the mirror to comb through her perfectly styled hair. A giant diamond flashes on her ring finger.

"I'm so impressed by you."

I briefly meet her eyes in the mirror as I grab a paper towel to dry my hands. "Sorry, what?"

"You're just so brave to wear that." She motions to my bodysuit and high-waisted jeans. "You don't see that style on most women because it's really hard to pull off unless you're a size zero. *I* can't even wear it. But it's awesome that you're doing whatever the hell you want and rocking it anyway."

I don't know what to say. From her tone, I can tell she genuinely thinks she's giving me a compliment instead of a thinly veiled insult about how my plus-sized body doesn't belong in the fashion I choose. It's not like this sort of comment is new to me, but still. It hits like a splash of icy water against my newly kindled confidence.

My cheeks flame. All I can do is nod and flee the bathroom.

Main character energy. Main character energy. You are a beautiful badass author, I think desperately as I walk back to my computer. *You will not let some bimbo in a bathroom take that away from you.*

The screen swims before my eyes. I blink rapidly, trying to pull it together.

Out of the corner of my eye, I see the blonde walk out of the bathroom and toward the table with the two kids. She rests her hand on the dark-haired dad's shoulder and leans in. The song playing over the speakers ends at the same moment, and sound travels easily in the quiet room.

"Vaughn, do you want another drink?"

My blood runs cold. The man turns away from the kids and to the blonde at his side, and the profile leaves no doubt. Vaughn, here at the bar. With this model and her—their?—two children.

What in the actual fuck?

I thought he just owed some money. But he has a family too? A wife? And yet he's taking me out to waterfalls and leading me on like some sort of idiot? Maybe he *didn't* even have a shift at the bar yesterday. Maybe he had to meet his *family*.

Realizing I don't actually know anything about this man I was imagining a future with feels like a physical blow to the chest. And God, he must have seen my text by now. Was he just sitting there, feet away from me, thinking about how pathetic I am?

All the oxygen flees the room, leaving me gasping. Whatever I thought was between us, I clearly couldn't have been more wrong.

I need to get out of this place. I slam my laptop shut and am sliding off my barstool when a familiar smiling man appears behind the bar.

"Landon! It's so great to see you!" Aaron booms as if we're old friends.

I flinch, eyes immediately darting back to Vaughn. His shoulders stiffen. He turns. His intense gaze, the one that normally sends chills of a different kind down my spine, hits me like an arctic blast.

Even after our conversation yesterday, even knowing he doesn't want to continue seeing me, the expression on his face shocks me. It's not just disdain or disinterest. It's so much darker.

What did I do to deserve this? When *he* was the one lying the whole damn time?

He stands and says something in a low voice to the beautiful blonde. The woman who is clearly all the things I'll never be.

Quickly, I grab the last few dollars out of my wallet and drop the money on the counter.

"You're not staying?" Aaron asks. He clearly has no idea what's going on. His eyes flick between Vaughn and me.

The words won't come. I can only shake my head, grab my things, and race out the door.

Of all the bad dates I've been on in my life, never have I been so wrong about a man. I know it's only been a couple days, but I was falling for the broody bartender. I thought he saw me, appreciated me, felt the same. Even today, a flicker of hope that things would work out still burned in my chest. I thought whatever happened yesterday was a fluke that could be resolved if I just took a shot.

Not anymore.

He doesn't want me.

10

VAUGHN

"WHAT THE HECK WAS that about?" Aaron studies me, eyes narrowed.

I walk to the bar on wooden legs. The front door still creaks from Landon's hasty departure. I don't know what to say. How can I possibly explain everything that happened in the last twenty-four hours?

And what the hell was she doing here? She was the last person I expected to see.

I stall, pulling my phone out of my pocket and checking to see if I have any notifications. My stomach drops another foot when I see two texts from Landon.

Before I can read them, Aaron prods. "Well? I thought you two hit it off, but you just looked at her like she murdered your dog. What's the deal? Was it really that bad of a date yesterday?"

Before I respond, I tap to open Landon's messages.

> *Hey Vaughn. I don't know what happened yesterday, if it was your phone call that changed things, or if it was me. But honestly, I don't care. I think there's something here between us, and I'll regret it if I don't take a shot at it. So here I am, asking you to give me one more chance. Because things like this don't come along often, and I'm ready for something extraordinary. With you.*

> *And if that isn't what you want, I understand—AND what I said yesterday still stands. I'm here for you if you need help, if you want me to be.*

Shame-fueled chills spiral from the base of my neck all the way down to my toes. I drop my head into my hands and groan.

I've spent all day fighting off tidal waves of emotion. First, absolute fury at my dad. Then, a sucker punch of thoughts about Landon. Guilt at my behavior. Misery at what I lost by ending things. Fiery anger at my dad once more. Panic about what the hell I'm going to do next.

The moment I get one emotion under control, the next pops up. It's like playing Whac-A-Mole with my insides.

And after my disappointing conversation with Katya over the last hour, I've been barely holding back the urge to smash something for real.

The sound of Landon's name brought up yet another rush of rage and guilt and grief. And even though none of it was *directed* at her—I didn't even know she was there—all that wrath was evidently written all over my face.

How would she know that it wasn't *at* her?

Add that on top of her text, and I can't even imagine how she must feel right now. She asked *me* out. She fought for me, even though I was a huge asshole yesterday. She was bold. She was perfect.

She *is* perfect.

And she probably thinks I just ignored her because I don't feel the same. When of course, she's done nothing but make my heart grow. Given how horrified she looked when she raced out, I'll probably never get the chance to tell her that fundamental truth.

But nothing's changed, and being with me would only make her life worse. I'm like the Grinch, only my heart keeps shrinking now that she's gone.

My adam's apple bobs as I try to get rid of the horrible blade that has settled in my throat. "I'm in trouble, man."

"I can see that. Do you think Landon thinks Katya and you are, you know, together? That those are your kids? Maybe she thinks you have a secret family or something."

I didn't think I could feel worse until that moment.

Fuck. Does Landon think that too? Is she questioning everything that happened yesterday now? Does she think I was leading her on? Probably, given how abruptly I ended things with no explanation. She doesn't deserve this, not from me. Not after all the shit other men have put her through.

That feeling of wanting to punch through a window comes back in full force.

I let out a low growl of frustration and anger. "Thank you for planting that idea, but that's not even the worst of it. I'm in deep shit right now."

I tell Aaron about my dad, the loan, and my new Friday deadline.

"He called right as Landon and I were leaving the restaurant. I can't have her involved in any of this. One, it could be dangerous. And two, she would never want to be with a deadbeat like me. At this rate, I'll be homeless within the week. I had to stop it before she got her hopes up."

Before *I* got my hopes up is more accurate, but I can't say it.

Aaron doesn't say anything to me. He just looks down the bar and calls, "Javi? Can you take over for a bit? The rush shouldn't hit for a while yet."

The other bartender pauses restocking the shelves to nod an affirmative and flash a thumbs-up.

Aaron comes out from behind the bar. "Come on, let's get out of here for a bit."

"I'm with Katya and the kids, I should—"

"She's their mom. They'll be just fine without you. I'm assuming she already turned you down for a loan?" Aaron asks.

I don't know how he could possibly know that, but I nod.

"Yeah, big surprise," he says, sarcasm dripping from his voice.

I frown at him.

Aaron continues, "I'm sorry, but she's been using you for years. I know you love those kids, and they love you, but it doesn't mean their mom is the best human. It doesn't surprise me at all that she's not there for you when the chips are down."

He doesn't even lower his voice. For all I know, Katya can hear every word from where she's sitting with the kids. Though, realistically, she's probably just scrolling social media on her phone and ignoring everyone else. But what surprises me more than Aaron's total lack of concern about being overheard is that I've never heard him say *anything* negative about … well, anyone, I don't think.

He grabs my arm and steers me to the back exit. "Bye, Katya, ladies. I'm taking Uncle Vaughn out for a bit. Javi will grab the check for you," he calls to my cousin. The girls pause in their napkin-coloring to wave. Katya, on the other hand, stares coldly up at us from the table. Her glossed lips part to speak, but we're already ducking through the door.

Aaron and I put on our gear and mount up. He motions for me to follow him and speeds off down the road.

It only takes about five minutes before I know exactly where we're heading. The old railroad overpass.

Back in high school, Aaron and I discovered a small dirt path that took us right onto the abandoned train tracks. It was only a short walk from there to the bridge over the river. It became our spot. Not only was it always a thrill being up so high on the rickety old overpass, but it also gave us a great place to drink beer without getting caught. We still stop by once every year or so to have a beer and enjoy the sight of the sprawling mountains and rushing river below.

We navigate our bikes into the small dirt patch on the edge of the deserted road. We leave our helmets on the seats and set off down the path. When we arrive at the bridge, Aaron walks fearlessly over the creaking structure to the middle and lowers himself slowly into a seated position. He grimaces down at his leg, which I know must be bothering him. I take the space beside him without comment, though, and give him a moment to adjust.

I dangle my legs over the edge and stare out at the forest in the direction of Temptation Falls, knowing that the tiny town is nestled just out of sight. Landon's there somewhere, hating me. The storm clouds gathering in the sky match my mood.

"I'm sorry," Aaron says finally. "You don't deserve all the shit your dad puts you through."

I don't say anything.

"I know you're going to roll your eyes when I say this—or maybe punch me in the face—but I do see a silver lining in all of this. I mean, look, this week is going to suck. I wish I had the money to help, but Sullivan's is barely staying afloat as it is after everything."

I make to interrupt. Aaron was in an accident a year ago. Not only did he get seriously injured, but his dad didn't make it out alive. Sullivan's place passed to Aaron, and since getting out of his physical rehabilitation program, he's been working his ass off to get the place up and running again. I'd never take a damn dime from him.

Aaron waves me off. "I know, I know, you would never ask me. But you're like a brother to me, man. I'll do anything in my power to help you. That's why we're going to figure this out together, somehow. We'll find a solution."

I don't know how to articulate how much those simple words make my chest ache. The offer of help from someone who already has so much on his plate. An offer with no strings attached.

Aaron's been my friend for years, but … I think I forgot what that meant. With my mom gone and everything going on with my dad, I've felt so alone for so long. I haven't had family to stick by me. Unless I count Katya and her kids, but when was the last time Katya offered to help me? Use me as a minimum-wage babysitter, sure, but invite me for a family dinner? Not once. And when I asked her to help me out today, her rejection was immediate.

The simple idea that I have someone in my corner, even when shit hits the fan, means more to me than I could ever have predicted.

My thoughts stray back to yesterday. To Landon offering to help me figure it all out, without even knowing what she was getting into. To her telling me I didn't need to do it all alone. The lump rises in my throat again.

Maybe there are people in this world who can be trusted.

Aaron goes on, "Once we find a solution, you're done. You don't have to worry anymore about that loan. I know it's been eating you alive. But you can just *be done.* Do whatever you want. Build whatever you want. Yeah, you're going to be a bit cash-poor, but you'll make it back. Remember, you're my best fruity-drink maker. I can't possibly let you out of a job so easily."

"I don't know how you always stay so freaking optimistic," I finally reply, elbowing him in the side. "But yeah, I guess you're right. I just need to get my hands on ten grand."

"We'll figure that part out when we get back to the bar. Right now, though, I want to talk about something else."

A furrow forms on my brow. "Please don't drop some other horrible news on me. I don't think I can take it."

"No, it's about Landon."

Yeah, I definitely can't take this right now.

I start to argue, but Aaron interrupts me. "Just let me get this out. Over the last few years, all you've done is work. I know why, and it makes total sense, but I'm seriously worried about you, man. It's not just that you're working all the time—it's that you've seemed so shut down. Walled off. When's the last time you even went on a date?"

I can't remember.

"When Landon came in last week, I saw the old you flickering through again. Yeah, you were an awkward, possessive, alpha-wannabe mess, but you were *reacting* to something for a change. You didn't have to go chase after her when she left on Saturday, but you did. You actually left a work shift to go because there's something there. I could feel it sparking between you two. That's the kind of thing you only get a few times in life, if you're lucky. So, why in the hell would you let that go?"

Words desert me. I've built these walls so gradually for so long that I didn't think anyone else noticed. And Aaron's words about Landon are true. I *felt* something, something strong, for the first time in a long time. Only now I've gone and screwed it all up.

"What if I can't pay this debt, Aaron? What if my dad does drop my name to whatever bad news he's mixed up in? What if Landon gets dragged into it all?"

"We're going to figure out the money, you have my word. Even if we have to shake it out of Katya as repayment for all that babysitting. Or we can ask the guys—you know they'd help you in a heartbeat. So, if that concern is off the table, what's holding you back?"

That she won't want me now. That I can't take care of her. That she'll leave me for someone better.

But I can't say any of that out loud.

Aaron seems to understand my silence. He claps me on the shoulder. "Do you like this girl?"

Finally, I actually know the answer to one of Aaron's questions.

"I don't just *like* this girl, man. She's fucking perfect," I growl.

"Then that's it. Let's go get her."

"I can't. I ruined all of it. She's never going to want to see me again," I say.

Aaron takes a moment to adjust his position before carefully rising to a stand, forcing me to twist my head to squint up at him.

"Are you going to cheat on this girl? Hurt her? Gamble away her savings? Put her in danger?"

"God, of course not. Why the hell would you ask me that?"

"To remind you that you're a good man, even if you're an idiot sometimes. Yeah, it sounds like you made a mistake. But you also just had a huge shock, and you have this massive thing hanging over your head. So, it's time to man up. That means owning up to what you did while still forgiving yourself for it, and going to find this girl to make it up to her. If what you're feeling is the real deal—"

"It is," I cut in. I might not know anything else about my life for certain right now, but I know that.

"—then go get her."

I don't realize I'm moving until I'm standing right in front of Aaron. Without a word, I hug my friend. Then, I say, "I'm going to get her back."

Aaron grins. "See, all it takes for a man to see sense is a Harley ride, a scenic view, and a bro intervention."

We turn to walk back to our bikes. An idea clicks into place.

I know what I need to do to get the money and finish this fucking thing.

"I need to make a few stops."

11

LANDON

MY EYES WON'T FOCUS, even though my book is open and ready to be read. So, instead, I stare into space as I nurse my glass of wine.

I stopped crying hours ago, but now I just feel empty. The sound of rain beating the pavement outside only adds to my gloomy mood.

So much for main character energy.

But even as the dark thought crosses my mind, I stop myself. That isn't right, is it?

Main character energy has been incredible for me. I made progress on a book. I built a friendship with Maya. I felt beautiful in my own skin and stood straight and proud. I had an amazing time with Vaughn, and even if it didn't end like I wanted, I had more fun talking about books and exploring a new place with him than I'd had in ages.

I took the damn shot—and I'm proud of myself for it.

In just a few days, a bunch of things have actually gone *right*.

Even that kiss ... that kiss was worth all the tears.

I *am* a badass author. I *am* gorgeous and worthy of love. I *am* going to finish my book and get it published. I am certainly *not* going to let myself doubt my own worth again.

Hell yes for main character energy.

Despite all the good, though, my heart still aches about Vaughn. In just a few days, he stole a piece of my heart. I've never experienced this level of pull toward a man, never had someone make my toes curl with only a look.

But if he's not going to treat me the way I deserve, if he's not going to love on the same level as I do, then I don't want him.

Maybe things with Vaughn aren't meant to be—and that has to be okay.

I drink the rest of my wine and stand. A bubble bath and face mask are definitely in order. As I walk to the bathroom, though, a knock startles me.

Frowning, I pad to the door and look through the peephole.

My breath catches. Vaughn stands in the hallway.

What is he doing here?

I quickly comb my hair with shaking fingers and glance down at my body. I swapped out my cute outfit for loungewear as soon I got home, not expecting to see anyone else tonight. I'm not even wearing a bra, and I'm sure my face is swollen. But nothing to be done now. I sigh and steel myself.

I open the door.

He towers before me in that familiar leather jacket. His sodden hair drips rainwater, and he clutches a package in his hands.

"Hi," he says in that gruff and gravel voice I could listen to all day.

My body reacts to his presence against my will, familiar molten heat pooling deep in my stomach. "Hi."

"I'm going to try to get this all out in one go, okay?" he says.

I tilt my head in confusion but nod. He takes a deep breath.

"Look, I fucked up, and I'm so sorry for it. I never should have ended things like that. That phone call really messed with my head. And I took it out on you, like an asshole. I didn't know how to do this thing between us with everything else going on. I was trying to protect you from all my shit, but you don't deserve to be treated like that. These two days with you have been the best time I've had in years. Literally, *years.* That first moment I saw you in the bar ... I knew it had to be you."

Vaugh scrubs his hand over his beard. My heart beats a staccato rhythm against my rib cage.

He goes on, "I know it hasn't been long, but you are the single most incredible woman I've ever met. You're gorgeous. You're smart. You're creative. You're way out of my league. I never should have let you go yesterday. I don't want to let you go at all. So, I'm here, asking you for another chance. I may be broke and even a bit broken, but I'll do everything in my fucking power to make you happy. Because you're right—I think we can be extraordinary."

He saw my text. I close my eyes for a brief moment as I try to gather myself, then I meet his piercing gaze.

"Please. I'm asking for one more chance," he says.

I can't squeeze any words past the lump in my throat.

He holds the package out to me. Tentatively, I remove the damp plastic bag to reveal a wrapped gift. I know immediately that it's a book. My trembling fingers peel away the patterned paper.

Zen and the Art of Motorcycle Maintenance. A first edition hardback.

My chest rises and falls like an ocean swell. He's only known me for two days, and he's picked the perfect gift. Flowers, chocolates, jewelry—those gifts mean nothing to me. But *this*.

I run one finger over the smooth edge of the cover, tracing the letters of the title.

"I know it's not much, but you said it was one of your favorites ... "

"It's not much?" I say incredulously. "Do you not realize how much this means?"

"I know you like nice things. I wish I could get you something nicer, but I just can't afford—"

"There are a lot of definitions of 'nice things.' The ones that matter are the ones that *mean* something. Do you really think I would care more about getting something expensive?"

He rubs at his beard again. "My head just isn't on straight, I don't think. You said yesterday you like nice things, and my first thought was that I can't provide them for you. I fucking hated that feeling."

"Vaughn, if I want a nice pair of shoes, I'm going to buy them for myself, okay? Because they make me feel good, and I earn them. I make more than enough money to support myself. I'm not one of those girls that needs to get showered with purses and other crap just for the hell of it." I hold up the book. "This is by far the most perfect gift I could ever have imagined. I hope you can believe that."

He nods slowly, like the wheels of his brain are trying to click into place. "Okay. Good." After a silent moment stretches between us, he goes on, "I think we've gotten sidetracked, though. Where are we on that one-more-chance thing?" His familiar gentle growl brings goosebumps to my skin.

But there's still a dark shadow hanging over my decision.

"Who was that woman earlier? Whose kids were those?" I blurt.

Vaughn cracks a small, crooked smile. "My cousin and her kids."

"Your cousin?"

"Yes."

An exhale escapes me in a whoosh, and the tension lifts from my shoulders. I hug the book to my chest. "Well, that's a relief. If that had been your wife, I would've been so disappointed in you."

He takes a step closer. "Is that a yes to that second chance?"

"Just one final question."

"Anything."

"Why are you wet?"

His laugh makes my heart stutter. "I had to walk here. And I don't know if you've noticed, but it's pissing down rain. Getting caught in these storms seems to be a habit of ours."

My eyebrows knit together. "Okay, wait. One more question. Where's your bike?"

He looks at the floor. "I sold it."

"For the ten grand?"

Vaughn's chin snaps up. "How do you know about that?"

"You said something about it on the phone yesterday. About owing money. Should I be concerned?"

He shakes his head forcefully. "No. I owed money to my dad for paying my law school tuition. He's not a good guy, and I think he got into some trouble recently. I had to get him the rest of the money. So, I brought the bike into the shop where I go for parts, and the owner snapped it up. He's been eyeing it for years. I just transferred my dad the money. It's all done. And I'm all done with him."

Reaching out, I rest my hand on his arm. "I'm sorry."

"I'm not. This loan has been hanging over my head for three years. It's all I've thought about day and night. I'm fucking *free*. I don't have to keep feeling like shit every time I get a call from my dad. I get to choose what happens in my life from here on out."

His eyes grow molten, and he takes another step closer until we're only inches apart. "I've got a pretty good idea of what I'd like to do next, if you'll let me."

It's like my fingertips have a mind of their own. They trail their way up his muscular arm, roam to his chest. I dip my hand under the edge of his damp leather jacket, laying my palm flat on his hard pec. The feel of his heartbeat is palpable through the thin fabric of his T-shirt.

His hand rises to rest over mine, forming a shield of intertwined fingers over his heart. The space between us grows charged, making me hyperaware of my own skin. Of the distance between our bodies.

Slowly, Vaughn steps forward, using his body to back me into my apartment, giving me plenty of time to say no. But it's the last word on my mind.

The door slams shut behind us. Somehow, the book falls onto the entryway table, and his other hand finds my waist. And then we're against the wall, Vaughn's massive body caging me in.

"Landon," he growls, looking down at me with those dark, magnetic eyes. The sound of my name in his mouth makes me shiver. "I need you to say it. Say you're giving me that chance."

"Yes—" is all I can get out before his mouth closes on mine.

He doesn't just kiss me.

He devours me.

His tongue sweeps in and massages my own until every nerve in my body is aflame. His mouth moves to my neck, nipping and quickly kissing away the sting. Rough fingers explore, trace the collarbone exposed by my oversized sweater, feel the soft edges of my hips, drift down to squeeze my ass. And I can't get enough of it.

Massive hands rise to cup my jaw, tilting my head so he can find the perfect angle for our mouths to slant together.

I moan into him, and he presses his hips tighter against mine to pin me against the wall. A denim-clad knee finds its way between my thighs, pushing up just enough to create a delicious friction that makes me writhe. My head spins with the scent of him, soap and leather and his own unique musk. I tangle my fingers in his wavy hair, not caring that the water droplets fall like small pricks of ice on our feverish skin.

He growls again and, without warning, lifts me up. For a moment, I'm scared he won't be able to hold me—but the fear is short lived. My legs wrap tightly around his torso, trying to pull him even closer. He carries me down the hall to my bedroom, never breaking contact with my mouth.

He gently lays me down on the bed and braces his huge frame above me. I stroke his short beard, run my fingers through his hair once more. He leans into my touch as he stares down into my eyes.

"Where are those boots?" he whispers.

"What boots?"

"The boots from yesterday. The ones that come all the way ... up ... here ..." he traces his finger up my leg with every word, until his hand comes to rest on my thigh.

"In the closet," I breathe.

"Too far away," he murmurs regretfully. "But I'm getting those out later." His voice is full of promise.

His lips find mine again.

Our bodies are fire, burning hotter and hotter for each other. One hand finds my breast. I can feel his rough callouses as he cups the sensitive flesh for a moment before gently pinching at my nipple, sending a zinging sensation straight down to my core. I gasp, but he kisses away my breath. He moves to the other side and teases the peaked flesh.

I can feel how hard he is for me, straining against his jeans, and it turns me on even more. But between the taste of his mouth and the overwhelming sensations wrought by his hands, I can't form words to tell him how much I need him.

The hand that's been so tortuously playing with my breasts slides down. His fingers come to rest on my hip and squeeze, just a few inches away from where I so desperately need them to be.

Vaughn's leather jacket is gone, torn off at some point in the frenzy, and I tug at his shirt, needing to see his skin, needing to feel it. He rises to his knees for a moment and pulls it over his head to reveal a broad, muscled chest. A tattoo sleeve starts at his left forearm, wraps all the way to his shoulder, and splashes across his pec. Another piece spans his right ribcage.

I sit up with him still straddling me. With a tentative finger, I trace the ink, like I've wanted to do since the first moment I saw it in the bar.

The sound he makes is pure desire, and it's like gas on our flame. Our mouths collide, and his hands find the edge of my sweater. He pulls back a moment, evaluating my response. I can only nod and lift my arms to let him remove the single piece of fabric that separates my skin from his.

Immediately, his lips go to my breasts, licking and sucking and bringing me to a heat that I didn't know was possible.

I lie back to give him better access. His fingers go straight to my waistline. He tugs the leggings ever so slowly down my thighs, planting kisses with every inch of revealed skin. I hear the fabric drop to the floor in a heap. The only piece of clothing left is my underwear. Everything else is exposed. To him.

I'm panting hard. My fingers tangle in his hair to gently tug him closer. But he slows, rising slightly and splaying his huge hands across my torso.

"What? What's wrong?" I say.

Vaughn presses a kiss against the flesh of my stomach. His breath hot against my skin, he whispers, "You're so fucking beautiful."

At those four simple words, my heart explodes. That he can see all of me and find it all beautiful means more than words can ever explain. I'm falling deeper and deeper into this feeling, this unbreakable bond that's taking shape between us.

His fingers travel lower until they brush the silk of my thong. He nudges aside the sheer panel of fabric to find my slick folds. I whimper at his touch, and he pauses again.

"Should we stop?" he pants. "We can go slow. Whatever you want."

"Don't you dare fucking stop."

He smiles at the growl in my own voice. His fingers start to move, slowly thrusting in and out before curling up to find that spot that makes me gasp and writhe. I grip his arm with one hand, leaving claw marks, while my other hand clutches at the bed, trying to keep from floating away on this pleasure.

My back arches as he hits a particularly sensitive spot. "Please, I need more. I need you, Vaughn. Please," I beg.

"You sure?" he breathes against my ear, still playing with me. "I bet I can make this really, really good for you, just like this."

"Please. I need you. Now," I gasp.

"As you wish," he says, adding a final stroke that elicits another whimper. He pulls his fingers away and raises them to his mouth. He tastes them. Tastes *me*. He gives me a wicked grin. "So fucking delicious."

Before I can react, he drags my panties down my legs and tosses them away. I lie before him, fully exposed, fully vulnerable, fully ready. He pauses as his eyes drag up my body, drinking me in. "Fucking gorgeous," he mutters. "Don't you dare move."

He pulls a small metal foil from his wallet before removing his own jeans and briefs to reveal the hard length of him. Seeing Vaughn's entire body is a shock, from the muscles to the tattoos to the defined V-line muscles pointing right ... there. I lick my lips and stare for a moment. He's huge, and he's ready for me. *Because* of me.

It sends even more electricity to my center, and I can't wait any longer. As soon as he slides the condom on, I wrap a leg over his waist and tug him down desperately.

He slides into me, and a cry escapes my mouth. He pauses to let me adjust to his size.

"Are you going to take all of me, baby?"

"Yes. God, yes," I gasp.

"Fucking right, you are," Vaughn growls in my ear.

He pushes in even deeper until his hard cock is fully sheathed. My muscles flex around him as I try to get used to the fullness.

One hand fondles my breasts again, playing with my peaked nipples, and he kisses me roughly. I melt into all the tantalizing feelings, and everything else clicks into perfect place. He starts to move. His rhythm is steady, even, and the pressure in my core builds, an endless rising mountain of sensation that makes me clutch him tighter. It's perfect, and yet it's not enough. I need more.

"Harder. Please, I need it harder, Vaughn."

"Oh, I'll give you harder, baby."

If I thought he had fully sheathed himself before, I was wrong. His thrusts turn almost punishing, driving into me as I clutch the headboard behind me with one hand. My legs spread wider to take him, and I can't get enough of it. My hips flex up to meet his and take him even deeper with every stroke. Every time he plunges in, he nudges my clit, carrying me even higher.

His teeth find the sensitive skin between my neck and collarbone and bite.

At the jolt of pain against so much overwhelming pleasure, I'm blown away. My vision fades to stars, an aftershock of sensation rocking through me. The waves of my orgasm keep crashing, over and over, like nothing I've ever felt before. Distantly, I hear him grunt as he releases, his body tightening as he rides his own pleasure. A moment later, his sweat-slicked body collapses over mine even as he stays buried inside me.

For a minute, I can't move. I've never felt so delicious in my entire life.

Vaughn finally pulls out, takes care of the condom, and rolls to lie by my side, propped up on one elbow as he runs his fingers over my collarbone, my breasts, down the curve of my stomach. He leans over to kiss me. We explore with our tongues once more, the longing just as acute as it was in our first embrace.

After an age, the kiss slows. Our breath is still ragged. His lips trail down my neck, beard scratching at the hypersensitive skin. I let out an involuntary laugh at the tickle. He grins into my throat.

"Fuck, these curves are gonna be the death of me, aren't they?" he whispers, his hot breath warming my ear. He follows the words with a small nip to my earlobe that makes my toes curl.

"But won't it be a way to go," I finish, biting my swollen lip as I gaze up at this man.

At *my* man.

"The best fucking way to go," he replies.

Epilogue: Vaughn

I SIT IN THE booth at the back of Sullivan's Place, waiting. My hand itches to go to my jacket pocket, but instead, I drum my fingers impatiently on the table.

Other patrons flock to the bar. It's packed. A year ago, I would've been hustling for the extra cash, taking the shift on a busy night no matter how exhausted I was. Now, I'm content to let Aaron and Javier handle it. By the looks of it, the crowd of women can't get enough of the pair. Aaron glances in my direction and gives me a jolly wink before spinning a liquor bottle with a flourish, earning gasps from the ladies. I smile despite myself.

The door to the bar swings open, and my heart leaps. Landon strolls in, arm in arm with her friend Maya. I immediately get to my feet and wave them over, greeting

Maya with a smile before planting a soft kiss on Landon's lips.

It's been six months, and the wanting never stops. This woman has undone me and remade me into a new, better man. A man who lets people in. A man who trusts. A man who can let his guard down, be present in the moment, and even have some fun.

Even though the finances were sticky for a while after paying my dad, I pulled through, just like Aaron said I would. And Landon hasn't cared for a second that I don't treat her to fancy dinners or gifts—yet. She seems to love my disastrous attempts at cooking as much as our evenings having discounted bar food at Sullivan's. When we're together, it's simple. And fucking hot.

I haven't heard from my dad once since wiring him the rest of the loan. Yeah, part of me is hurt, but the other, bigger part of me is just relieved. I deserve better, and I have it now. Actually, I have more than better. I have the best fucking woman in the world by my side, and I'm never going to let her go.

I make to slide back into the booth, but Landon holds my arm.

"Hang on a second, babe." She beams at me. "I actually have some news."

"And it's freaking awesome!" Maya interjects, grinning at us before taking my seat at the booth and stealing a gulp of my beer.

"What?"

"I did it."

I cock an eyebrow at her, waiting for her to clarify.

"I made the bestseller list."

"What!" My shout draws the attention of every person in the bar, but I don't give a damn. "Are you serious? Tell me you're serious."

"I'm serious. I did it!"

I pick her up and spin her. "That's amazing! Congratulations, baby! You fucking deserve it."

"I can't believe it's really happening." Landon nearly dances in my arms, her face so bright and happy that my heart swells in my chest like a great balloon. "And to imagine, it's all because I met this broody bartender who inspired me to try out writing romance."

"And because of that great best friend who told you to keep writing and encouraged you to publish the damn thing yourself!" Maya calls over her shoulder. "Don't forget about us peasants now that you're a big-shot author!"

Landon turns to Maya. "Hell yes, girl. You were a vital part of this journey too." But her sparkling eyes find mine again. "I love you," she says softly.

The words make me glow every single time.

"I love you. I'm so proud of you, Landon."

"Thank you. But ... I've actually got one more thing too. Will you come outside with me for a second?"

Suddenly, she's oddly hesitant. What is this all about?

"Sure, yeah. What's up?" I ask.

"I'd rather show you, if it's okay."

I interlace my fingers with hers. "Of course it's okay. Let's go."

Leaving Maya behind with my beer, I trail Landon as she exits the bar and walks to the corner.

"Do you trust me?" she says.

"Of course," I reply without hesitation.

"Then close your eyes." Her own brilliant blue eyes are huge as they look up at me. She's nervous. Why the hell is she nervous?

"Why?"

"Just do it!" She swats me on the arm, and though I frown at her, I oblige. I'd follow this woman blindfolded into a volcano if she asked me to.

She tugs at me, guiding me around the corner for a few more steps. My boots scrape over the rough pavement, and I clutch her small hand tighter.

We come to a stop. I hear her take a deep breath, so I give her fingers a comforting squeeze.

"Okay. You can open your eyes now."

I blink. Landon stands off to my side, biting her lip as she looks up at me. My eyes fall to what's just behind her.

A sleek black Harley sits in the alley. A very familiar Harley. *My* Harley. The one I sold to pay back my dad. I'd know it anywhere.

"How?" I choke out.

"Aaron helped. We were able to convince the guy you sold it to that he could have something even better instead. He let me buy it back."

"You bought this? For me?" My eyes burn.

She nods, studying my face nervously. "Do you like it?"

"I can't let you do this. It's too much," I grind out.

"It's not. And it's already done. If you don't take it, I'll have to sell it on eBay or something because I'm not learning how to drive it."

I can only stare at her. Her face softens into a gentle smile.

"Consider it your cut of the book. You deserve a little something for all the research you helped me do." Her smile turns into a sly smirk. "And there's all that work you're going to have to help with for the sequel. Lots of good kissing scenes we need to block out to see if the flow makes sense. This is your advance for your trouble."

The woman has the nerve to wink at me.

"You're serious?"

"I'm serious. But you have to take me for a ride soon, okay?"

"Oh, baby, I'll take you for a ride," I say huskily, the promise clear. But then I grow serious again. "Landon, I don't even know what to say. No one has ever done something like this for me. Just ... thank you. So much."

She stands on her tiptoes and kisses me, slow and deep. I grip her waist, craving the feel of her body against mine.

How did I get so fucking lucky to have her?

There will never be a rational answer. I can never deserve this woman. But I damn well will spend the rest of my life trying.

The box in my jacket pocket burns against my skin. I wanted to wait, wanted to do something big and romantic. Not be in an alley outside a bar.

But if I don't act right now, my heart will explode.

So I break our kiss and take a step away from Landon.

She frowns, reaching out to me in confusion. Until I drop to one knee and pull out the small velvet box.

My hands shake as I flip it open to reveal the solitary diamond set in a white gold band. I've been carrying around my mother's ring for two months now, biding my time. I didn't want to seem too desperate.

But I don't give a shit about seeming too desperate anymore. I *am* desperate, for God's sake. I should give a speech, tell her all the reasons why I love her, explain that I'll cherish her until the day I die. But there will be time for that later. Right now, I just need to know if she'll be mine forever.

"Will you marry me?"

Landon's mouth falls open, her hands rising to her face. Those soft blonde waves blow in the breeze, lips flushed from my kisses, and I don't think I've ever seen anyone more beautiful. That I would kneel before no matter what.

"Are you serious?" she says, so quietly I can barely hear her.

I nod, holding her gaze. "I'm serious. I want to marry you. More than I've ever wanted anything in my entire life. Will you have me?"

The next moment is the longest I've ever experienced in my life.

"Yes! God, yes. I'll marry you," she cries, launching herself into my arms and smothering my face with kisses. I rise and lift her off the ground to swing us in a circle. I kiss her back with wild joy pulsing through my entire body.

"Yes, yes, yes," Landon keeps repeating between kisses. I didn't think I could be any happier, but each time she says the word yes, my euphoria mounts.

Finally, I set her down and take her hand. Pulling the ring from the box, I slip it over her finger. She looks at it, eyes alight.

"Do you like it?" I ask.

"It's perfect. Absolutely perfect."

"It was my mother's ring. She told me to give it to my soulmate when I found her."

Landon's eyes fill with tears. "Thank you," she whispers, cradling the ring tight with her other hand for a moment. "I'll cherish it for the rest of my life. Just like I'll cherish you. I love you so much."

"I fucking love you, baby. Now, let's go celebrate. And luckily, I know just the place for free drinks."

And, I want the world to see that this woman is *mine*.

Mine. Forever and always.

THANK YOU FOR READING!

D ID YOU ENJOY *A Shot at Love*? If so, GREAT news. You can get a free, exclusive BONUS scene when you subscribe to my newsletter! **Scan the QR code below to start reading:**

www.kaysinclair.com/

ashotatlove-qr

(If you already get my newsletter, you'll still need to enter your email one more time. But don't worry, you won't get double emails after that!)

This bonus scene is a sneak peek into Landon and Vaughn's life a few years down the road, and I can't wait for you to read it.

Plus, once you sign up, you'll have exclusive access to other freebies and be the first to know about new releases! You'll also get to know a little more about me, Kay Sinclair—and I hope I can get to know you too. Building connections with my readers is one of my favorite parts of being an author.

One more thing before you go. If you fell in love with Landon and Vaughn, I hope you'll consider taking a couple of minutes to **leave a review.** Reviews make a huge difference for indie authors like me; every review helps my books get seen by the right readers. I would be extremely grateful if you'd consider writing one.

Want more of Temptation Falls?

You can find all the available books by scanning the QR code on the last page, or by heading here: www.kaysinclair.com/books.

No cheating. No cliffhangers. Just sweet and sexy stories about curvy women—happily ever afters guaranteed.

Thanks for reading, and I hope to see you again soon!

About the Author

KAY SINCLAIR IS A romance author who writes short and sexy stories about curvy women and the hunky heroes who fall for them.

When she's not writing or taking long, meandering walks through the forest with her dog, Kay can be found sipping cappuccinos in a coffee shop or enjoying a good novel by the fireplace on a rainy day. You can find her at www.kaysinclair.com or on Facebook at www.facebook.com/authorkaysinclair.